DOVER · THRIFT

First Love
and
The Diary of a Superfluous Man

IVAN TURGENEV

DOVER PUBLICATIONS, INC.
New York

DOVER THRIFT EDITIONS

General Editor: Stanley Appelbaum
Editor of This Volume: Philip Smith

Copyright

Published in Canada by General Publishing Company, Ltd., 30 Lesmill Road, Don Mills, Toronto, Ontario.
Published in the United Kingdom by Constable and Company, Ltd., 3 The Lanchesters, 162–164 Fulham Palace Road, London W6 9ER.

Bibliographical Note

This Dover edition, first published in 1995, contains the unabridged, slightly corrected texts of two works originally published in the series *The Novels of Ivan Turgenev*, translated by Constance Garnett. ("First Love" appeared in Volume XI, *The Torrents of Spring, Etc.* [1897] and "The Diary of a Superfluous Man" appeared in Volume XIII, *The Diary of a Superfluous Man, Etc.* [1899]. Both volumes were originally published by William Heinemann, London.) A new introductory Note and a few explanatory footnotes have been added to the present edition.

Library of Congress Cataloging-in-Publication Data

Turgenev, Ivan Sergeevich, 1818–1883.
[Pervaia liubov'. English]
First love ; and, The Diary of a superfluous man / Ivan Turgenev ; [translated by Constance Garnett].
p. cm. — (Dover thrift editions)
ISBN 0-486-28775-0 (pbk.)
1. Turgenev, Ivan Sergeevich, 1818–1883 — Translations into English. I. Garnett, Constance Black, 1862–1946. II. Turgenev, Ivan Sergeevich, 1818–1883. Dnevnik lishnego cheloveka. English. III. Title. IV. Title: Diary of a superfluous man. V. Series.
PG3421.P4E5 1995
891.73'3 — dc20 95-20126
CIP

Manufactured in the United States of America
Dover Publications, Inc., 31 East 2nd Street, Mineola, N.Y. 11501

Note

IVAN SERGEYEVICH TURGENEV (1818–1883) was widely viewed as Russia's greatest fiction writer during his lifetime. Although his writings have suffered comparative neglect during the twentieth century (which has favored the more agitated works of Tolstoy and Dostoyevsky), their impeccable craftsmanship and masterful evocations of character and place have found an enduring audience among lovers of literature around the world. Turgenev first attained literary prominence with a series of 22 short prose pieces collected as *A Sportsman's Sketches* in 1852. These were followed by a steady succession of notable works, including the play *A Month in the Country* (1855) and the novels *Rudin* (1856), *A Nest of Gentry* (1859), *On the Eve* (1860), *Fathers and Sons* (1862), *Smoke* (1867) and *Virgin Soil* (1877).

This volume contains two of Turgenev's greatest shorter works, the novellas *The Diary of a Superfluous Man* (1850) and *First Love* (1860). Both reflect their author's mastery of literary form and concern with the nuanced depiction of psychological states, as well as his genius for creating fictional situations that allow for the unfolding and revelation of characters' inmost depths.

Contents

The Diary of a Superfluous Man

VILLAGE OF SHEEP'S SPRINGS,
March 20, 18—.

THE doctor has just left me. At last I have got at something definite! For all his cunning, he had to speak out at last. Yes, I am soon, very soon, to die. The frozen rivers will break up, and with the last snow I shall, most likely, swim away . . . whither? God knows! To the ocean too. Well, well, since one must die, one may as well die in the spring. But isn't it absurd to begin a diary a fortnight, perhaps, before death? What does it matter? And by how much are fourteen days less than fourteen years, fourteen centuries? Beside eternity, they say, all is nothingness—yes, but in that case eternity, too, is nothing. I see I am letting myself drop into metaphysics; that's a bad sign—am I not rather faint-hearted, perchance? I had better begin a description of some sort. It's damp and windy out of doors. I'm forbidden to go out. What can I write about, then? No decent man talks of his maladies; to write a novel is not in my line; reflections on elevated topics are beyond me; descriptions of the life going on around me could not even interest me; while I am weary of doing nothing, and too lazy to read. Ah, I have it, I will write the story of all my life for myself. A first-rate idea! Just before death it is a suitable thing to do, and can be of no harm to any one. I will begin.

I was born thirty years ago, the son of fairly well-to-do landowners. My father had a passion for gambling; my mother was a woman of character . . . a very virtuous woman. Only, I have known no woman whose moral excellence was less productive of happiness. She was crushed beneath the weight of her own virtues, and was a source of misery to every one, from herself upwards. In all the fifty years of her life, she never once took rest, or sat with her hands in her lap; she was for ever fussing and bustling about like an ant, and to absolutely no good purpose, which cannot be said of the ant. The worm of restlessness fretted her night and day. Only once I saw her perfectly tranquil, and that was the day after her death, in her coffin. Looking at her, it positively seemed to me that her face wore an expression of subdued amazement; with the half-open lips, the sunken cheeks, and meekly-staring eyes, it seemed expressing, all over, the words, 'How good to be at rest!' Yes, it is good, good to be rid, at last, of the wearing sense of life, of the persistent, restless consciousness of existence! But that's neither here nor there.

I was brought up badly and not happily. My father and mother both loved me; but that made things no better for me. My father was not, even in his own house, of the slightest authority or consequence, being a man openly abandoned to a shameful and ruinous vice; he was conscious of his degradation, and not having the strength of will to give up his darling passion, he tried at least, by his invariably amiable and humble demeanour and his unswerving submissiveness, to win the condescending consideration of his exemplary wife. My mother certainly did bear her trial with the superb and majestic long-suffering of virtue, in which there is so much of egoistic pride. She never reproached my father for anything, gave him her last penny, and paid his debts without a word. He exalted her as a paragon to her face and behind her back, but did not like to be at home, and caressed me by stealth, as though he were afraid of contaminating me by his presence. But at such times his distorted features were full of such kindness, the nervous grin on his lips was replaced by such a touching smile, and his brown eyes, encircled by fine wrinkles, shone with such love, that I could not help pressing my cheek to his, which was wet and warm with tears. I wiped away those tears with my handkerchief, and they flowed again without effort, like water from a brimming glass. I fell to crying, too, and he comforted me, stroking my back and kissing me all over my face with his quivering lips. Even now, more than twenty years after his death, when I think of my poor father, dumb sobs rise into my throat, and my heart beats as hotly and bitterly and aches with as poignant a pity as if it had long to go on beating, as if there were anything to be sorry for!

My mother's behaviour to me, on the contrary, was always the same, kind, but cold. In children's books one often comes across such mothers, sermonising and just. She loved me, but I did not love her. Yes! I fought shy of my virtuous mother, and passionately loved my vicious father.

But enough for to-day. It's a beginning, and as for the end, whatever it may be, I needn't trouble my head about it. That's for my illness to see to.

March 21.

To-day it is marvellous weather. Warm, bright; the sunshine frolicking gaily on the melting snow; everything shining, steaming, dripping; the sparrows chattering like mad things about the drenched, dark hedges. Sweetly and terribly, too, the moist air frets my sick chest. Spring, spring is coming! I sit at the window and look across the river into the open country. O nature! nature! I love thee so, but I came forth from thy womb good for nothing — not fit even for life. There goes a cock-sparrow, hopping along with outspread wings; he chirrups, and every note, every ruffled feather on his little body, is breathing with health and strength. . . .

What follows from that? Nothing. He is well and has a right to chirrup and ruffle his wings; but I am ill and must die—that's all. It's not worth while to say more about it. And tearful invocations to nature are mortally absurd. Let us get back to my story.

I was brought up, as I have said, very badly and not happily. I had no brothers or sisters. I was educated at home. And, indeed, what would my mother have had to occupy her, if I had been sent to a boarding-school or a government college? That's what children are for—that their parents may not be bored. We lived for the most part in the country, and sometimes went to Moscow. I had tutors and teachers, as a matter of course; one, in particular, has remained in my memory, a dried-up, tearful German, Rickmann, an exceptionally mournful creature, cruelly maltreated by destiny, and fruitlessly consumed by an intense pining for his far-off fatherland. Sometimes, near the stove, in the fearful stuffiness of the close ante-room, full of the sour smell of stale kvas, my unshaved man-nurse, Vassily, nicknamed Goose, would sit, playing cards with the coachman, Potap, in a new sheepskin, white as foam, and superb tarred boots, while in the next room Rickmann would sing, behind the partition—

'Herz, mein Herz, warum so traurig?
Was bekümmert dich so sehr?
'S ist ja schön im fremden Lande—
Herz, mein Herz—was willst du mehr?'[1]

After my father's death we moved to Moscow for good. I was twelve years old. My father died in the night from a stroke. I shall never forget that night. I was sleeping soundly, as children generally do; but I remember, even in my sleep, I was aware of a heavy gasping noise at regular intervals. Suddenly I felt some one taking hold of my shoulder and poking me. I opened my eyes and saw my nurse. 'What is it?' 'Come along, come along, Alexey Mihalitch is dying.' . . . I was out of bed and away like a mad thing into his bed-room. I looked: my father was lying with his head thrown back, all red, and gasping fearfully. The servants were crowding round the door with terrified faces; in the hall some one was asking in a thick voice: 'Have they sent for the doctor?' In the yard outside, a horse was being led from the stable, the gates were creaking, a tallow candle was burning in the room on the floor, my mother was there, terribly upset, but not oblivious of the proprieties, nor of her own dignity. I flung myself on my father's bosom, and hugged him, faltering: 'Papa, papa . . .' He lay motionless, screwing up his

[1] *'Herz, . . . mehr?'*] "Heart, my heart, why so sad? What troubles you so much? It is beautiful, after all, in this strange land—heart, my heart, what more do you want?"

eyes in a strange way. I looked into his face—an unendurable horror caught my breath; I shrieked with terror, like a roughly captured bird—they picked me up and carried me away. Only the day before, as though aware his death was at hand, he had caressed me so passionately and despondently.

A sleepy, unkempt doctor, smelling strongly of spirits, was brought. My father died under his lancet, and the next day, utterly stupefied by grief, I stood with a candle in my hands before a table, on which lay the dead man, and listened senselessly to the bass sing-song of the deacon, interrupted from time to time by the weak voice of the priest. The tears kept streaming over my cheeks, my lips, my collar, my shirt-front. I was dissolved in tears; I watched persistently, I watched intently, my father's rigid face, as though I expected something of him; while my mother slowly bowed down to the ground, slowly rose again, and pressed her fingers firmly to her forehead, her shoulders, and her chest, as she crossed herself. I had not a single idea in my head; I was utterly numb, but I felt something terrible was happening to me. . . . Death looked me in the face that day and took note of me.

We moved to Moscow after my father's death for a very simple cause: all our estate was sold up by auction for debts—that is, absolutely all, except one little village, the one in which I am at this moment living out my magnificent existence. I must admit that, in spite of my youth at the time, I grieved over the sale of our home, or rather, in reality, I grieved over our garden. Almost my only bright memories are associated with our garden. It was there that one mild spring evening I buried my best friend, an old bobtailed, crook-pawed dog, Trix. It was there that, hidden in the long grass, I used to eat stolen apples—sweet, red, Novgorod apples they were. There, too, I saw for the first time, among the ripe raspberry bushes, the housemaid Klavdia, who, in spite of her turned-up nose and habit of giggling in her kerchief, aroused such a tender passion in me that I could hardly breathe, and stood faint and tongue-tied in her presence; and once at Easter, when it came to her turn to kiss my seignorial hand, I almost flung myself at her feet to kiss her down-trodden goat-skin slippers. My God! Can all that be twenty years ago? It seems not long ago that I used to ride on my shaggy chestnut pony along the old fence of our garden, and, standing up in the stirrups, used to pick the two-coloured poplar leaves. While a man is living he is not conscious of his own life; it becomes audible to him, like a sound, after the lapse of time.

Oh, my garden, oh, the tangled paths by the tiny pond! Oh, the little sandy spot below the tumbledown dike, where I used to catch gudgeons! And you tall birch-trees, with long hanging branches, from beyond which came floating a peasant's mournful song, broken by the uneven jolting of the cart, I send you my last farewell! . . . On parting with life, to you alone I stretch out my hands. Would I might once more inhale the fresh, bitter fragrance of the wormwood, the sweet scent of the mown buckwheat in the fields of my native place! Would I might once more hear far away the modest tinkle of the cracked bell of our parish church; once more lie in the cool shade under the oak sapling on the slope of the familiar ravine; once more watch the moving track of the wind, flitting, a dark wave over the golden grass of our meadow! . . . Ah, what's the good of all this? But I can't go on to-day. Enough till to-morrow.

March 22.

To-day it's cold and overcast again. Such weather is a great deal more suitable. It's more in harmony with my task. Yesterday, quite inappropriately, stirred up a multitude of useless emotions and memories within me. This shall not occur again. Sentimental outbreaks are like liquorice; when first you suck it, it's not bad, but afterwards it leaves a very nasty taste in the mouth. I will set to work simply and serenely to tell the story of my life. And so, we moved to Moscow. . . .

But it occurs to me, is it really worth while to tell the story of my life?

No, it certainly is not. . . . My life has not been different in any respect from the lives of numbers of other people. The parental home, the university, the government service in the lower grades, retirement, a little circle of friends, decent poverty, modest pleasures, unambitious pursuits, moderate desires — kindly tell me, is that new to any one? And so I will not tell the story of my life, especially as I am writing for my own pleasure; and if my past does not afford even me any sensation of great pleasure or great pain, it must be that there is nothing in it deserving of attention. I had better try to describe my own character to myself. What manner of man am I? . . . It may be observed that no one asks me that question — admitted. But there, I'm dying, by Jove! — I'm dying, and at the point of death I really think one may be excused a desire to find out what sort of a queer fish one really was after all.

Thinking over this important question, and having, moreover, no need whatever to be too bitter in my expressions in regard to myself, as people are apt to be who have a strong conviction of their valuable qualities, I must admit one thing. I was a man, or perhaps I should say a fish, utterly superfluous in this world. And that I propose to show to-morrow, as I keep coughing to-day like an old sheep, and my nurse, Terentyevna, gives me no peace: 'Lie down, my good sir,' she says, 'and drink a little tea.' . . . I know why she keeps on at me: she wants some tea herself. Well! she's welcome! Why not let the poor old woman extract the utmost benefit she can from her master at the last . . . as long as there is still the chance?

March 23.

Winter again. The snow is falling in flakes. Superfluous, superfluous. . . . That's a capital word I have hit on. The more deeply I probe into myself, the more intently I review all my past life, the more I am convinced of the strict truth of this expression. Superfluous—that's just it. To other people that term is not applicable. . . . People are bad, or good, clever, stupid, pleasant, and disagreeable; but superfluous . . . no. Understand me, though: the universe could get on without those people too . . . no doubt; but uselessness is not their prime characteristic, their most distinctive attribute, and when you speak of them, the word 'superfluous' is not the first to rise to your lips. But I . . . there's nothing else one can say about me; I'm superfluous and nothing more. A supernumerary, and that's all. Nature, apparently, did not reckon on my appearance, and consequently treated me as an unexpected and uninvited guest. A facetious gentleman, a great devotee of preference, said very happily about me that I was the forfeit my mother had paid at the game of life. I am speaking about myself calmly now, without any bitterness. . . . It's all over and done with!

Throughout my whole life I was constantly finding my place taken, perhaps because I did not look for my place where I should have done. I was apprehensive, reserved, and irritable, like all sickly people. Moreover, probably owing to excessive self-consciousness, perhaps as the result of the generally unfortunate cast of my personality, there existed between my thoughts and feelings, and the expression of those feelings and thoughts, a sort of inexplicable, irrational, and utterly insuperable barrier; and whenever I made up my mind to overcome this obstacle by force, to break down this barrier, my gestures, the expression of my face, my whole being, took on an appearance of painful constraint. I not only seemed, I positively became unnatural and affected. I was conscious of this myself, and hastened to shrink back into myself. Then a terrible commotion was set up within me. I analysed myself to the last thread, compared myself with others, recalled the slightest glances, smiles, words of the people to whom I had tried to open myself out, put the worst construction on everything, laughed vindictively at my own pretensions to 'be like every one else,'—and suddenly, in the midst of my laughter, collapsed utterly into gloom, sank into absurd dejection, and then began again as before—went round and round, in fact, like a squirrel on its wheel. Whole days were spent in this harassing, fruitless exercise. Well now, tell me, if you please, to whom and for what is such a man of use? Why did this happen to me? what was the reason of this trivial fretting at myself?—who knows? who can tell?

I remember I was driving once from Moscow in the diligence. It was a good road, but the driver, though he had four horses harnessed abreast, hitched on another, alongside of them. Such an unfortunate, utterly useless, fifth horse—fastened somehow on to the front of the shaft by a short stout cord, which mercilessly cuts his shoulder, forces him to go with the most unnatural action, and gives his whole body the shape of a comma—always arouses my deepest pity. I remarked to the driver that I thought we might on this occasion have got on without the fifth horse. . . . He was silent a moment, shook his head, lashed the horse a dozen times across his thin back and under his distended belly, and with a grin responded: 'Ay, to be sure; why do we drag him along with us? What the devil's he for?' And here am I too dragged along. But, thank goodness, the station is not far off.

Superfluous. . . . I promised to show the justice of my opinion, and I will carry out my promise. I don't think it necessary to mention the thousand trifles, everyday incidents and events, which would, however, in the eyes of any thinking man, serve as irrefutable evidence in my support—I mean, in support of my contention. I had better begin straight away with one rather important incident, after which probably there will be no doubt left of the accuracy of the term superfluous. I repeat: I do not intend to indulge in minute details, but I cannot pass over in silence one rather serious and significant fact, that is, the strange behaviour of my friends (I too used to have friends) whenever I met them, or even called on them. They used to seem ill at ease; as they came to meet me, they would give a not quite natural smile, look, not into my eyes nor at my feet, as some people do, but rather at my cheeks, articulate hurriedly, 'Ah! how are you, Tchulkaturin!' (such is the surname fate has burdened me with) or 'Ah! here's Tchulkaturin!' turn away at once and positively remain stockstill for a little while after, as though trying to recollect something. I used to notice all this, as I am not devoid of penetration and the faculty of observation; on the whole I am not a fool; I sometimes even have ideas come into my head that are amusing, not absolutely commonplace. But as I am a superfluous man with a padlock on my inner self, it is very painful for me to express my idea, the more so as I know beforehand that I shall express it badly. It positively sometimes strikes me as extraordinary the way people manage to talk, and so simply and freely. . . . It's marvellous, really, when you think of it. Though, to tell the truth, I too, in spite of my padlock, sometimes have an itch to talk. But I did actually utter words only in my youth; in riper years I almost always pulled myself up. I would murmur to myself: 'Come, we'd better hold our tongue.' And I was still. We are all good hands at being silent; our women especially are great in that line. Many an exalted Russian young lady keeps silent so strenuously that the spectacle is calculated to produce a faint shudder and cold sweat even in any one prepared to face it. But that's not the point, and it's not for me to criticise others. I proceed to my promised narrative.

A few years back, owing to a combination of circumstances, very insignificant in themselves, but very important for me, it was my lot to spend six months in the district town O——. This town is all built on a slope, and very uncomfortably built, too. There are reckoned to be about eight hundred inhabitants in it, of exceptional poverty; the houses are hardly worthy of the name; in the chief street, by way of an apology for a pavement, there are here and there some huge white slabs of rough-hewn limestone, in consequence of which even carts drive round it instead of through it. In the very middle of an astoundingly dirty square rises a diminutive yellowish edifice with black holes in it, and in these holes sit men in big caps making a pretence of buying and selling. In this place there is an extraordinarily high striped post sticking up into the air, and near the post, in the interests of public order, by command of the authorities, there is kept a cartload of yellow hay, and one government hen struts to and fro. In short, existence in the town of O—— is truly delightful. During the first days of my stay in this town, I almost went out of my mind with boredom. I ought to say of myself that, though I am, no doubt, a superfluous man, I am not so of my own seeking; I'm morbid myself, but I can't bear anything morbid. . . . I'm not even averse to happiness—indeed, I've tried to approach it right and left. . . . And so it is no wonder that I too can be bored like any other mortal. I was staying in the town of O—— on official business.

Terentyevna has certainly sworn to make an end of me. Here's a specimen of our conversation:—

TERENTYEVNA. Oh—oh, my good sir! what are you for ever writing for? it's bad for you, keeping all on writing.

I. But I'm dull, Terentyevna.

SHE. Oh, you take a cup of tea now and lie down. By God's mercy you'll get in a sweat and maybe doze a bit.

I. But I'm not sleepy.

SHE. Ah, sir! why do you talk so? Lord have mercy on you! Come, lie down, lie down; it's better for you.

I. I shall die any way, Terentyevna!

SHE. Lord bless us and save us! . . . Well, do you want a little tea?

I. I shan't live through the week, Terentyevna!

SHE. Eh, eh! good sir, why do you talk so? . . . Well, I'll go and heat the samovar.

Oh, decrepit, yellow, toothless creature! Am I really, even in your eyes, not a man?

March 24. *Sharp frost.*

On the very day of my arrival in the town of O——, the official business, above referred to, brought me into contact with a certain Kirilla Matveitch Ozhogin, one of the chief functionaries of the district; but I became intimate, or, as it is called, 'friends' with him a fortnight later. His house was in the principal street, and was distinguished from all the others by its size, its painted roof, and the lions on its gates, lions of that species extraordinarily resembling unsuccessful dogs, whose natural home is

Moscow. From those lions alone, one might safely conclude that Ozhogin was a man of property. And so it was; he was the owner of four hundred peasants; he entertained in his house all the best society of the town of O——, and had a reputation for hospitality. At his door was seen the mayor with his wide chestnut-coloured droshky and pair—an exceptionally bulky man, who seemed as though cut out of material that had been laid by for a long time. The other officials, too, used to drive to his receptions: the attorney, a yellowish, spiteful creature; the land surveyor, a wit—of German extraction, with a Tartar face; the inspector of means of communication—a soft soul, who sang songs, but a scandal-monger; a former marshal of the district—a gentleman with dyed hair, crumpled shirt-front, and tight trousers, and that lofty expression of face so characteristic of men who have stood on trial. There used to come also two landowners, inseparable friends, both no longer young and indeed a little the worse for wear, of whom the younger was continually crushing the elder and putting him to silence with one and the same reproach. 'Don't you talk, Sergei Sergeitch! What have you to say? Why, you spell the word cork with two *k*'s in it. . . . Yes, gentlemen,' he would go on, with all the fire of conviction, turning to the bystanders, 'Sergei Sergeitch spells it not cork, but kork.' And every one present would laugh, though probably not one of them was conspicuous for special accuracy in orthography, while the luckless Sergei Sergeitch held his tongue, and with a faint smile bowed his head. But I am forgetting that my hours are numbered, and am letting myself go into too minute descriptions. And so, without further beating about the bush,—Ozhogin was married, he had a daughter, Elizaveta Kirillovna, and I fell in love with this daughter.

Ozhogin himself was a commonplace person, neither good-looking nor bad-looking; his wife resembled an aged chicken; but their daughter had not taken after her parents. She was very pretty and of a bright and gentle disposition. Her clear grey eyes looked out kindly and directly from under childishly arched brows; she was almost always smiling, and she laughed too, pretty often. Her fresh voice had a very pleasant ring; she moved freely, rapidly, and blushed gaily. She did not dress very stylishly, only plain dresses suited her. I did not make friends quickly as a rule, and if I were at ease with any one from the first—which, however, scarcely ever occurred—it said, I must own, a great deal for my new acquaintance. I did not know at all how to behave with women, and in their presence I either scowled and put on a morose air, or grinned in the most idiotic way, and in my embarrassment turned my tongue round and round in my mouth. With Elizaveta Kirillovna, on the contrary, I felt at home from the first moment. It happened in this way.

I called one day at Ozhogin's before dinner, asked, 'At home?' was told, 'The master's at home, dressing; please to walk into the drawing-room.' I went into the drawing-room; I beheld standing at the window, with her back to me, a girl in a white gown, with a cage in her hands. I was, as my way was, somewhat taken aback; however, I showed no sign of it, but merely coughed, for good manners. The girl turned round quickly, so quickly that her curls gave her a slap in the face, saw me, bowed, and with a smile showed me a little box half full of seeds. 'You don't mind?' I, of course, as is the usual practice in such cases, first bowed my head, and at the same time rapidly crooked my knees, and straightened them out again (as though some one had given me a blow from behind in the legs, a sure sign of good breeding and pleasant, easy manners), and then smiled, raised my hand, and softly and carefully brandished it twice in the air. The girl at once turned away from me, took a little piece of board out of the cage, began vigorously scraping it with a knife, and suddenly, without changing her attitude, uttered the following words: 'This is papa's parrot. . . . Are you fond of parrots?' 'I prefer siskins,' I answered, not without some effort. 'I like siskins, too; but look at him, isn't he pretty? Look, he's not afraid.' (What surprised me was that I was not afraid.) 'Come closer. His name's Popka.' I went up, and bent down. 'Isn't he really sweet?' She turned her face to me; but we were standing so close together, that she had to throw her head back to get a look at me with her clear eyes. I gazed at her; her rosy young face was smiling all over in such a friendly way that I smiled too, and almost laughed aloud with delight. The door opened; Mr. Ozhogin came in. I promptly went up to him, and began talking to him very unconstrainedly. I don't know how it was, but I stayed to dinner, and spent the whole evening with them; and next day the Ozhogins' footman, an elongated, dull-eyed person, smiled upon me as a friend of the family when he helped me off with my overcoat.

To find a haven of refuge, to build oneself even a temporary nest, to feel the comfort of daily intercourse and habits, was a happiness I, a superfluous man, with no family associations, had never before experienced. If anything about me had had any resemblance to a flower, and if the comparison were not so hackneyed, I would venture to say that my soul blossomed from that day. Everything within me and about me was suddenly transformed! My whole life was lighted up by love, the whole of it, down to the paltriest details, like a dark, deserted room when a light has been brought into it. I went to bed, and got up, dressed, ate my breakfast, and smoked my pipe—differently from before. I positively skipped along as I walked, as though wings were suddenly sprouting from my shoulders. I was not for an instant, I remember, in uncertainty with regard to the feeling Elizaveta Kirillovna inspired in me. I fell passionately in love with her from the first day, and from the first day I knew I was in love. During the course of three weeks I saw her every day. Those three weeks were the happiest time in my life; but the recollection of them is painful to me. I can't think of them alone; I cannot help dwelling on what followed after them, and the intensest bitterness slowly takes possession of my softened heart.

When a man is very happy, his brain, as is well known, is not very active. A calm and delicious sensation, the sensation of satisfaction, pervades his whole being; he is swallowed up by it; the consciousness of personal life vanishes in him—he is in beatitude, as badly educated poets say. But when, at last, this 'enchantment' is over, a man is sometimes vexed and sorry that, in the midst of his bliss, he observed himself so little; that he did not, by reflection, by recollection, redouble and prolong his feelings . . . as though the 'beatific' man had time, and it were worth his while to reflect on his sensations! The happy man is what the fly is in the sunshine. And so it is that, when I recall those three weeks, it is almost impossible for me to retain in my mind any exact and definite impression, all the more so as during that time nothing very remarkable took place between us. . . . Those twenty days are present to my imagination as something warm, and young, and fragrant, a sort of streak of light in my dingy, greyish life. My memory becomes all at once remorselessly clear and trustworthy, only from the instant when, to use the phrase of badly-educated writers, the blows of destiny began to fall upon me.

Yes, those three weeks. . . . Not but what they have left some images in my mind. Sometimes when it happens to me to brood a long while on that time, some memories suddenly float up out of the darkness of the past—like stars which suddenly come out against the evening sky to meet the eyes straining to catch sight of them. One country walk in a wood has remained particularly distinct in my memory. There were four of us, old Madame Ozhogin, Liza, I, and a certain Bizmyonkov, a petty official of the town of O——, a light-haired, good-natured, and harmless person. I shall have more to say of him later. Mr. Ozhogin had stayed at home; he had a headache, from sleeping too long. The day was exquisite; warm and soft. I must observe that pleasure-gardens and picnic-parties are not to the taste of the average Russian. In district towns, in the so-called public gardens, you never meet a living soul at any time of the year; at the most, some old woman sits sighing and moaning on a green garden seat, broiling in the sun, not far from a sickly tree—and that, only if there is no greasy little bench in the gateway near. But if there happens to be a scraggy birchwood in the neighbourhood of the town, tradespeople and even officials gladly make excursions thither on Sundays and holidays, with samovars, pies, and melons; set all this abundance on the dusty grass, close by the road, sit round, and eat and drink tea in the sweat of their brows till evening. Just such a wood there was at that time a mile and a half from the town of O——. We repaired there after dinner, duly drank our fill of tea, and then all four began to wander about the wood. Bizmyonkov walked with Madame Ozhogin on his arm, I with Liza on mine. The day was already drawing to evening. I was at that time in the very fire of first love (not more than a fortnight had passed since our first meeting), in that condition of passionate and concentrated adoration, when your whole soul innocently and unconsciously follows every movement of the beloved being, when you can never have enough of her presence, listen enough to her voice, when you smile with the look of a child convalescent after sickness, and a man of the smallest experience cannot fail at the first glance to recognise a hundred yards off what is the matter with you. Till that day I had never happened to have Liza on my arm. We walked side by side, stepping slowly over the green grass. A light breeze, as it were, flitted about us between the white stems of the birches, every now and then flapping the ribbon of her hat into my face. I incessantly followed her eyes, until at last she turned gaily to me and we both smiled at each other. The birds were chirping approvingly above us, the blue sky peeped caressingly at us through the delicate foliage. My head was going round with excess of bliss. I hasten to remark, Liza was not a bit in love with me. She liked me; she was never shy with any one, but it was not reserved for me to trouble her childlike peace of mind. She walked arm in arm with me, as she would with a brother. She was seventeen then. . . . And meanwhile, that very evening, before my eyes, there began that soft inward ferment which precedes the metamorphosis of the child into the woman. . . . I was witness of that transformation of the whole being, that guileless bewilderment, that agitated dreaminess; I was the first to detect the sudden softness of the glance, the sudden ring in the voice — and oh, fool! oh, superfluous man! For a whole week I had the face to imagine that I, I was the cause of this transformation!

This was how it happened.

We walked rather a long while, till evening, and talked little. I was silent, like all inexperienced lovers, and she, probably, had nothing to say to me. But she seemed to be pondering over something, and shook her head in a peculiar way, as she pensively nibbled a leaf she had picked. Sometimes she started walking ahead, so resolutely . . . then all at once stopped, waited for me, and looked round with lifted eyebrows and a vague smile. On the previous evening we had read together *The Prisoner of the Caucasus.*[1] With what eagerness she had listened to me, her face propped in both hands, and her bosom pressed against the table! I began to speak of our yesterday's reading; she flushed, asked me whether I had given the parrot any hempseed before starting, began humming some little song aloud, and all at once was silent again. The copse ended on one side in a rather high and abrupt precipice; below coursed a winding stream, and beyond it, over an immense expanse, stretched the boundless prairies, rising like waves, spread-

[1] *The Prisoner of the Caucasus*] i.e., *Kavkazkii plennik*, an 1822 poem by Russian poet, short-story writer and dramatist Aleksandr Pushkin.

ing wide like a table-cloth, and broken here and there by ravines. Liza and I were the first to come out at the edge of the wood; Bizmyonkov and the elder lady were behind. We came out, stood still, and involuntarily we both half shut our eyes; directly facing us, across a lurid mist, the vast, purple sun was setting. Half the sky was flushed and glowing; red rays fell slanting on the meadows, casting a crimson reflection even on the side of the ravines in shadow, lying in gleams of fire on the stream, where it was not hidden under the overhanging bushes, and, as it were, leaning on the bosom of the precipice and the copse. We stood, bathed in the blazing brilliance. I am not capable of describing all the impassioned solemnity of this scene. They say that by a blind man the colour red is imagined as the sound of a trumpet. I don't know how far this comparison is correct, but really there was something of a challenge in this glowing gold of the evening air, in the crimson flush on sky and earth. I uttered a cry of rapture and at once turned to Liza. She was looking straight at the sun. I remember the sunset glow was reflected in little points of fire in her eyes. She was overwhelmed, deeply moved. She made no response to my exclamation; for a long while she stood, not stirring, with drooping head. . . . I held out my hand to her, she turned away from me, and suddenly burst into tears. I looked at her with secret, almost delighted amazement. . . . The voice of Bizmyonkov was heard a couple of yards off. Liza quickly wiped her tears and looked with a faltering smile at me. The elder lady came out of the copse leaning on the arm of her flaxen-headed escort; they, in their turn, admired the view. The old lady addressed some question to Liza, and I could not help shuddering, I remember, when her daughter's broken voice, like cracked glass, sounded in reply. Meanwhile the sun had set, and the afterglow began to fade. We turned back. Again I took Liza's arm in mine. It was still light in the wood, and I could clearly distinguish her features. She was confused, and did not raise her eyes. The flush that overspread her face did not vanish; it was as though she were still standing in the rays of the setting sun. . . . Her hand scarcely touched my arm. For a long while I could not frame a sentence; my heart was beating so violently. Through the trees there was a glimpse of the carriage in the distance; the coachman was coming at a walking pace to meet us over the soft sand of the road.

'Lizaveta Kirillovna,' I brought out at last, 'what did you cry for?'

'I don't know,' she answered, after a short silence. She looked at me with her soft eyes still wet with tears—her look struck me as changed, and she was silent again.

'You are very fond, I see, of nature,' I pursued. That was not at all what I meant to say, and the last words my tongue scarcely faltered out to the end. She shook her head. I could not utter another word. . . . I was waiting for something ... not an avowal—how was that possible? I waited for a confiding glance, a question. . . . But Liza looked at the ground, and kept silent. I repeated once more in a whisper: 'Why was it?' and received no reply. She had grown, I saw that, ill at ease, almost ashamed.

A quarter of an hour later we were sitting in the carriage driving to the town. The horses flew along at an even trot; we were rapidly whirled along through the darkening, damp air. I suddenly began talking, more than once addressing first Bizmyonkov, and then Madame Ozhogin. I did not look at Liza, but I could see that from her corner in the carriage her eyes did not once rest on me. At home she roused herself, but would not read with me, and soon went off to bed. A turning-point, that turning-point I have spoken of, had been reached by her. She had ceased to be a little girl, she too had begun . . . like me . . . to wait for something. She had not long to wait.

But that night I went home to my lodgings in a state of perfect ecstasy. The vague half presentiment, half suspicion, which had been arising within me, had vanished. The sudden constraint in Liza's manner towards me I ascribed to maidenly bashfulness, timidity. . . . Hadn't I read a thousand times over in many books that the first appearance of love always agitates and alarms a young girl? I felt supremely happy, and was already making all sorts of plans in my head.

If some one had whispered in my ear then: 'You're raving, my dear chap! that's not a bit what's in store for you. What's in store for you is to die all alone, in a wretched little cottage, amid the insufferable grumbling of an old hag who will await your death with impatience to sell your boots for a few coppers . . .'!

Yes, one can't help saying with the Russian philosopher—'How's one to know what one doesn't know?'

Enough for to-day.

March 25. *A white winter day.*

I have read over what I wrote yesterday, and was all but tearing up the whole manuscript. I think my story's too spun out and too sentimental. However, as the rest of my recollections of that time present nothing of a pleasurable character, except that peculiar sort of consolation which Lermontov had in view when he said there is pleasure and pain in irritating the sores of old wounds, why not indulge oneself? But one must know where to draw the line. And so I will continue without any sort of sentimentality.

During the whole of the week after the country excursion, my position was in reality in no way improved, though the change in Liza became more noticeable every day. I interpreted this change, as I have said before, in the most favourable way for me. . . . The misfortune of solitary and timid people—who are timid from self-consciousness—is just that, though they have eyes and indeed open them wide, they see nothing, or see everything in a false light, as though through coloured spectacles. Their own ideas and speculations trip them up at every step. At the commencement of our acquaintance, Liza behaved confidingly and freely with me, like a child; perhaps there may even have been in her attitude to me something more than mere childish liking. . . . But after this strange, almost instantaneous change had taken place in her, after a period of brief perplexity, she felt constrained in my presence; she unconsciously turned away from me, and was at the same time melancholy and dreamy. . . . She was waiting . . . for what? She did not know . . . while I . . . I, as I have said above, was delighted at this change. . . . Yes, by God, I was ready to expire, as they say, with rapture. Though I am prepared to allow that any one else in my place might have been deceived. . . . Who is free from vanity? I need not say that all this was only clear to me in the course of time, when I had to lower my clipped and at no time over-powerful wings.

The misunderstanding that had arisen between Liza and me lasted a whole week—and there is nothing surprising in that: it has been my lot to be a witness of misunderstandings that have lasted for years and years. Who was it said, by the way, that truth alone is powerful? Falsehood is just as living as truth, if not more so. To be sure, I recollect that even during that week I felt from time to time an uneasy gnawing astir within me . . . but solitary people like me, I say again, are as incapable of understanding what is going on within them as what is taking place before their eyes. And, besides, is love a natural feeling? Is it natural for man to love? Love is a sickness; and for sickness there is no law. Granting that there was at times an unpleasant pang in my heart; well, everything inside me was turned upside down. And how is one to know in such circumstances, what is all right and what is all wrong? and what is the cause, and what the significance, of each separate symptom? But, be that as it may, all these misconceptions, presentiments, and hopes were shattered in the following manner.

One day—it was in the morning about twelve o'clock—I had hardly entered Mr. Ozhogin's hall, when I heard an unfamiliar, mellow voice in the drawing-room, the door opened, and a tall and slim man of five-and-twenty appeared in the doorway, escorted by the master of the house. He rapidly put on a military overcoat which lay on the slab, and took cordial leave of Kirilla Matveitch. As he brushed past me, he carelessly touched his foraging cap, and vanished with a clink of his spurs.

'Who is that?' I asked Ozhogin.

'Prince N.,' the latter responded, with a preoccupied face; 'sent from Petersburg to collect recruits. But where are the servants?' he went on in a tone of annoyance; 'no one handed him his coat.'

We went into the drawing-room.

'Has he been here long?' I inquired.

'Arrived yesterday evening, I'm told. I offered him a room here, but he refused. He seems a very nice fellow, though.'

'Has he been long with you?'

'About an hour. He asked me to introduce him to Olimpiada Nikitishna.'

'And did you introduce him?'

'Of course.'

'And Lizaveta Kirillovna, too, did he . . .'

'He made her acquaintance, too, of course.'

I was silent for a space.

'Has he come here for long, do you know?'

'Yes, I believe he has to be here for a fortnight.'

And Kirilla Matveitch hurried away to dress. I walked several times up and down the drawing-room. I don't recollect that Prince N.'s arrival made any special impression on me at the time, except that feeling of hostility which usually possesses us on the appearance of any new person in our domestic circle. Possibly there was mingled with this feeling something too of the nature of envy — of a shy and obscure person from Moscow towards a brilliant officer from Petersburg. 'The prince,' I mused, 'is an upstart from the capital; he'll look down upon us. . . .' I had not seen him for more than an instant, but I had had time to perceive that he was good-looking, clever, and at his ease. After pacing the room for some time, I stopped at last before a looking-glass, pulled a comb out of my pocket, gave a picturesque carelessness to my hair, and, as sometimes happens, became suddenly absorbed in the contemplation of my own face. I remember my attention centred anxiously about my nose; the soft and undefined outlines of that feature afforded me no great satisfaction, when suddenly in the dark depths of the sloping mirror, which reflected almost the whole room, the door opened, and the slender figure of Liza appeared. I don't know why I did not stir, and kept the same expression on my face. Liza craned her head forward, looked intently at me, and raising her eyebrows, biting her lips, and holding her breath as any one does who is glad at not being noticed, she cautiously drew back and stealthily drew the door to after her. The door creaked slightly. Liza started and stood rooted to the spot . . . I still kept from stirring . . . she pulled the handle again and vanished. There was no possibility of doubt: the expression of Liza's face at the sight of my figure, that expression in which nothing could be detected except a desire to get away again successfully, to escape a disagreeable interview, the quick flash of delight I had time to catch in her eyes when she fancied she really had managed to creep away unnoticed — it all spoke too clearly; that girl did not love me. For a long, long while I could not take my eyes off that motionless, dumb door, which was once more a patch of white in the looking-glass. I tried to smile at my own long face — dropped my head, went home again, and flung myself on the sofa. I felt extraordinarily heavy at heart, so much so that I could not cry . . . and, besides, what was there to cry about . . . ? 'Is it possible?' I repeated incessantly, lying, as though I were murdered, on my back with my hands folded on my breast—'is it possible?' . . . Don't you think that's rather good, that 'is it possible?'

March 26. *Thaw.*

When, next day, after long hesitation and with a low sinking at my heart, I went into the Ozhogins' familiar drawing-room, I was no longer the same man as they had known during the last three weeks. All my old peculiarities, which I had begun to get over, under the influence of a new feeling, reappeared and took possession of me, like proprietors returning to their house. People of my sort are usually guided, not so much by positive facts, as by their own impressions: I, who no longer ago than the day before had been dreaming of the 'raptures of love returned,' was that day no less convinced of my 'unhappiness,' and was absolutely despairing, though I was not myself able to find any rational ground for my despair. I could not as yet be jealous of Prince N., and whatever his qualities might be, his mere arrival was not sufficient to extinguish Liza's good-will towards me at once. . . . But stay, was there any good-will on her part? I recalled the past. 'What of the walk in the wood?' I asked myself. 'What of the expression of her face in the glass?' 'But,' I went on, 'the walk in the wood, I think . . . Fie on me! my God, what a wretched creature I am!' I said at last, out loud. Of such sort were the unphrased, incomplete thoughts that went round and round a thousand times over in a monotonous whirl in my head. I repeat, I went back to the Ozhogins' the same hypersensitive, suspicious, constrained creature I had been from my childhood up. . . .

I found the whole family in the drawing-room; Bizmyonkov was sitting there, too, in a corner. Every one seemed in high good-humour; Ozhogin, in particular, positively beamed, and his first word was to tell me that Prince N. had spent the whole of the previous evening with them. Liza gave me a tranquil greeting. 'Oh,' said I to myself; 'now I understand why you're in such spirits.' I must own the prince's second visit puzzled me. I had not anticipated it. As a rule fellows like me anticipate everything in the world, except what is bound to occur in the natural order of things; I sulked and put on the air of an injured but magnanimous person; I tried to punish Liza by showing my displeasure, from which one must conclude I was not yet completely desperate after all. They do say that in some cases when one is really loved, it's positively of use to torment the adored one; but in my position it was indescribably stupid. Liza, in the most innocent way, paid no attention to me. No one but Madame Ozhogin observed my solemn taciturnity, and she inquired anxiously after my health. I replied, of course, with a bitter smile, that I was thankful to say I was perfectly well. Ozhogin continued to expatiate on the subject of their visitor; but noticing that I responded reluctantly, he addressed himself principally to Bizmyonkov, who was listening to him with great attention, when a servant suddenly came in, announcing the arrival of Prince N. Our host jumped up and ran to meet him; Liza, upon whom I at once turned an eagle eye, flushed with delight, and made as though she would move from her seat. The prince came in, all agreeable perfume, gaiety, cordiality. . . .

As I am not composing a romance for a gentle reader, but simply writing for my own amusement, it stands to reason I need not make use of the usual dodges of our respected authors. I will say straight out without further delay that Liza fell passionately in love with the prince from the first day she saw him, and the prince fell in love with her too — partly from having nothing to do, and partly from a propensity for turning women's heads, and also owing to the fact that Liza really was a very charming creature. There was nothing to be wondered at in their falling in love with each other. He had certainly never expected to find such a pearl in such a wretched shell (I am alluding to the God-forsaken town of O——), and she had never in her wildest dreams seen anything in the least like this brilliant, clever, fascinating aristocrat.

After the first courtesies, Ozhogin introduced me to the prince, who was very affable in his behaviour to me. He was as a rule very affable with every one; and in spite of the immeasurable distance between him and our obscure provincial circle, he was clever enough to avoid being a source of constraint to any one, and even to make a show of being on our level, and only living at Petersburg, as it were, by accident.

That first evening. . . . Oh, that first evening! In our happy days of childhood our teachers used to describe and set up before us as an example the manly fortitude of the young Spartan, who, having stolen a fox and hidden it under his tunic, without uttering one shriek let it devour all his entrails, and so preferred death itself to disgrace. . . . I can find no better comparison for my indescribable sufferings during the evening on which I first saw the prince by Liza's side. My continual forced smile and painful vigilance, my idiotic silence, my miserable and ineffectual desire to get away — all that was doubtless something truly remarkable in its own way. It was not one wild beast alone gnawing at my vitals; jealousy, envy, the sense of my own insignificance, and helpless hatred were torturing me. I could not but admit that the prince really was a very agreeable young man. . . . I devoured him with my eyes; I really believe I forgot to blink as usual, as I stared at him. He talked not to Liza alone, but all he said was of course really for her. He must have felt me a great bore. He most likely guessed directly that it was a discarded lover he had to deal with, but from sympathy for me, and also a profound sense of my absolute harmlessness, he treated me with extraordinary gentleness. You can fancy how this wounded me! In the course of the evening I tried, I remember, to smooth over my mistake. I positively (don't laugh at me, whoever you may be, who chance to look through these lines — especially as it was my last illusion . . .) . . . I, positively, in the midst of my different sufferings, imagined all of a sudden that Liza wanted to punish me for my haughty coldness at the beginning of my visit, that she was angry with me and only flirting with the prince from pique. . . . I seized my opportunity and with a meek but gracious smile, I went up to her, and muttered — 'Enough, forgive me, not that I'm afraid . . .' and suddenly, without awaiting her reply, I gave my features an extraordinarily cheerful and free-and-easy expression, with a set grin, passed my hand above my head in the direction of the ceiling (I wanted, I remember, to set my cravat straight), and was even on the point of pirouetting round on one foot, as though to say, 'All is over, I am happy, let's all be happy,' — I did not, however, execute this manœuvre, as I was afraid of losing my balance, owing to an unnatural stiffness in my knees. . . . Liza failed absolutely to understand me; she looked in my face with amazement, gave a hasty smile, as though she wanted to get rid of me as quickly as possible, and again approached the prince. Blind and deaf as I was, I could not but be inwardly aware that she was not in the least angry, and was not annoyed with me at that instant: she simply never gave me a thought. The blow was a final one. My last hopes were shattered with a crash, just as a block of ice, thawed by the sunshine of spring, suddenly falls into tiny morsels. I was utterly defeated at the first skirmish, and, like the Prussians at Jena, lost everything at once in one day. No, she was not angry with me! . . .

Alas, it was quite the contrary! She too — I saw that — was being swept off her feet by the torrent. Like a young tree, already half torn from the bank, she bent eagerly over the stream, ready to abandon to it for ever the first blossom of her spring and her whole life. A man whose fate it has been to be the witness of such a passion, has lived through bitter moments if he has loved himself and not been loved. I shall for ever remember that devouring attention, that tender gaiety, that innocent self-oblivion, that glance, still a child's and already a woman's, that happy, as it were flowering smile that never left the half-parted lips and glowing cheeks. . . . All that Liza had vaguely foreshadowed during our walk in the wood had come to pass now — and she, as she gave herself up utterly to love, was at once stiller and brighter, like new wine, which ceases to ferment because its full maturity has come. . . .

I had the fortitude to sit through that first evening and the subsequent evenings . . . all to the end! I could have no hope of anything. Liza and the prince became every day more devoted to each other . . . But I had absolutely lost all sense of personal dignity, and could not tear myself away from the spectacle of my own misery. I remember one day I tried not to go, swore to myself in the morning that I would stay at home, and at eight o'clock in the evening (I usually set off at seven) leaped up like a madman, put on my hat, and ran breathless into Kirilla Matveitch's drawing-room. My position was excessively absurd. I was obstinately silent; sometimes for whole days together I did not utter a sound. I was, as I have said already, never distinguished for eloquence; but now everything I had in my mind took flight, as it were, in the presence of the prince, and I was left bare and bereft. Besides, when I was alone, I set my wretched brain working so hard, slowly going over everything I had noticed or surmised during the preceding day, that when I went back to the Ozhogins' I scarcely had energy left to observe again. They treated me considerately, as a sick person; I saw that. Every morning I adopted some new, final resolution, for the most part painfully hatched in the course of a sleepless night. At one time I made up my mind to have it out with Liza, to give her friendly advice . . . but when I chanced to be alone with her, my tongue suddenly ceased to work, froze as it were, and we both, in great discomfort, waited for the entrance of some third person. Another time I meant to run away, of course for ever, leaving my beloved a letter full of reproaches, and I even one day began this letter; but the sense of justice had not yet quite vanished in me. I realised that I had no right to reproach any one for anything, and I flung what I had written in the fire. Then I suddenly offered myself up wholly as a sacrifice, gave Liza my benediction, praying for her happiness, and smiled in meek and friendly fashion from my corner at the prince. But the cruel-hearted lovers not only never thanked me for my self-sacrifice, they never even noticed me, and were, apparently, quite ready to dispense with my smiles and my blessings. . . . Then, in wrath, I suddenly flew into quite the opposite mood. I swore to myself, wrapping my cloak about me like a Spaniard, to rush out from some dark corner and stab my lucky rival, and with brutal glee I imagined Liza's despair. . . . But, in the first place, such corners were few in the town of O——; and, secondly—the wooden fence, the street lamp, the policeman in the distance. . . . No! in such corners it was somehow far more suitable to sell buns and oranges than to shed human blood. I must own that, among other means of deliverance, as I very vaguely expressed it in my colloquies with myself, I did entertain the idea of having recourse to Ozhogin himself . . . of calling the attention of that nobleman to the perilous situation of his daughter, and the mournful consequences of her indiscretion. . . . I even once began speaking to him on a certain delicate subject; but my remarks were so indirect and misty, that after listening and listening to me, he suddenly, as it were, waking up, rubbed his hand rapidly and vigorously all over his face, not sparing his nose, gave a snort, and walked away from me. It is needless to say that in resolving on this step I persuaded myself that I was acting from the most disinterested motives, was desirous of the general welfare, and was doing my duty as a friend of the house. . . . But I venture to think that even had Kirilla Matveitch not cut short my outpourings, I should in any case not have had courage to finish my monologue. At times I set to work with all the solemnity of some sage of antiquity, weighing the qualities of the prince; at times I comforted myself with the hope that it was all of no consequence, that Liza would recover her senses, that her love was not real love . . . oh, no! In short, I know no idea that I did not worry myself with at that time. There was only one resource which never, I candidly admit, entered my head: I never once thought of taking my life. Why it did not occur to me I don't know. . . . Possibly, even then, I had a presentiment I should not have long to live in any case.

It will be readily understood that in such unfavourable circumstances my manner, my behaviour with people, was more than ever marked by unnaturalness and constraint. Even Madame Ozhogin — that creature dull-witted from her birth up — began to shun me, and at times did not know in what way to approach me. Bizmyonkov, always polite and ready to do services, avoided me. I fancied even at that time that I had in him a companion in misfortune — that he too loved Liza. But he never responded to my hints, and altogether showed a reluctance to converse with me. The prince behaved in a very friendly way to him; the prince, one might say, respected him. Neither Bizmyonkov nor I was any obstacle to the prince and Liza; but he did not shun them as I did, nor look savage nor injured — and readily joined them when they desired it. It is true that on such occasions he was not conspicuous for any special mirthfulness; but his good-humour had always been somewhat subdued in character.

In this fashion about a fortnight passed by. The prince was not only handsome and clever: he played the piano, sang, sketched fairly well, and was a good hand at telling stories. His anecdotes, drawn from the highest circles of Petersburg society, always made a great impression on his audience, all the more so from the fact that he seemed to attach no importance to them. . . .

The consequence of this, if you like, simple accomplishment of the prince's was that in the course of his not very protracted stay in the town of O— he completely fascinated all the neighbourhood. To fascinate us poor dwellers in the steppes is at all times a very easy task for any one coming from higher spheres. The prince's frequent visits to the Ozhogins (he used to spend his evenings there) of course aroused the jealousy of the other worthy gentry and officials of the town. But the prince, like a clever person and a man of the world, never neglected a single one of them; he called on all of them; to every married lady and every unmarried miss he addressed at least one flattering phrase, allowed them to feed him on elaborately solid edibles, and to make him drink wretched wines with magnificent names; and conducted himself, in short, like a model of caution and tact. Prince N— was in general a man of lively manners, sociable and genial by inclination, and in this case incidentally from prudential motives also; he could not fail to be a complete success in everything.

Ever since his arrival, all in the house had felt that the time had flown by with unusual rapidity; everything had gone off beautifully. Papa Ozhogin, though he pretended that he noticed nothing, was doubtless rubbing his hands in private at the idea of such a son-in-law. The prince, for his part, managed matters with the utmost sobriety and discretion, when, all of a sudden, an unexpected incident . . .

Till to-morrow. To-day I'm tired. These recollections irritate me even at the edge of the grave. Terentyevna noticed to-day that my nose has already begun to grow sharp; and that, they say, is a bad sign.

March 27. Thaw continuing.

Things were in the position described above: the prince and Liza were in love with each other; the old Ozhogins were waiting to see what would come of it; Bizmyonkov was present at the proceedings — there was nothing else to be said of him. I was struggling like a fish on the ice, and watching with all my might, — I remember that at that time I set myself the task of preventing Liza at least from falling into the snares of a seducer, and consequently began paying particular attention to the maidservants and the fateful 'back stairs' — though, on the other hand, I often spent whole nights in dreaming with what touching magnanimity I would one day hold out a hand to the betrayed victim and say to her, 'The traitor has deceived thee; but I am thy true friend . . . let us forget the past and be happy!' — when sudden and glad tidings overspread the whole town. The marshal of the district proposed to give a great ball in honour of their respected guest, on his private estate Gornostaevka. All the official world, big and little, of the town of O—— received invitations, from the mayor down to the apothecary, an excessively emaciated German, with ferocious pretensions to a good Russian accent, which led him into continually and quite inappropriately employing racy colloquialisms. . . . Tremendous preparations were, of course, put in hand. One purveyor of cosmetics sold sixteen dark-blue jars of pomatum, which bore the inscription *à la jesmin.*[1] The young ladies provided themselves with tight dresses, agonising in the waist and jutting out sharply over the stomach; the mammas put formidable erections on their heads by way of caps; the busy papas were half dead with the bustle. The longed-for day arrived at last. I was among those invited. From the town to Gornostaevka was reckoned between seven and eight miles. Kirilla Matveitch offered me a seat in his coach; but I refused. . . . In the same way

[1] *à la jesmin*] Probably an incorrect attempt to convey "scented with jasmine."

children, who have been punished, wishing to pay their parents out, refuse their favourite dainties at table. Besides, I felt that my presence would be felt as a constraint by Liza. Bizmyonkov took my place. The prince drove in his own carriage, and I in a wretched little droshky, hired for an immense sum for this solemn occasion. I am not going to describe that ball. Everything about it was just as it always is. There was a band, with trumpets extraordinarily out of tune, in the gallery; there were country gentlemen, greatly flustered, with their inevitable families, mauve ices, viscous lemonade; servants in boots trodden down at heel and knitted cotton gloves; provincial lions with spasmodically contorted faces, and so on and so on. And all this little world was revolving round its sun — round the prince. Lost in the crowd, unnoticed even by the young ladies of eight-and-forty, with red pimples on their brows and blue flowers on the top of their heads, I stared incessantly, first at the prince, then at Liza. She was very charmingly dressed and very pretty that evening. They only twice danced together (it is true, he danced the mazurka with her); but it seemed, to me at least, that there was a sort of secret, continuous communication between them. Even while not looking at her, while not speaking to her, he was still, as it were, addressing her, and her alone. He was handsome and brilliant and charming with other people — for her sake only. She was apparently conscious that she was the queen of the ball, and that she was loved. Her face at once beamed with childlike delight and innocent pride, and was suddenly illuminated by another, deeper feeling. Happiness radiated from her. I observed all this. . . . It was not the first time I had watched them. . . . At first this wounded me intensely; afterwards it, as it were, touched me; but, finally, it infuriated me. I suddenly felt extraordinarily wrathful, and, I remember, was extraordinarily delighted at this new sensation, and even conceived a certain respect for myself. 'We'll show them we're not crushed yet,' I said to myself. When the first inviting notes of the mazurka sounded, I looked about me with composure, and with a cool and easy air approached a long-faced young lady with a red and shiny nose, a mouth that stood awkwardly open, as though it had come unbuttoned, and a scraggy neck that recalled the handle of a bass-viol. I went up to her, and, with a perfunctory scrape of my heels, invited her to the dance. She was wearing a dress of faded rosebud pink, not full-blown rose colour; on her head quivered a striped and dejected beetle of some sort on a thick bronze pin; and altogether this lady was, if one may so express it, soaked through and through with a sort of sour ennui and inveterate lack of success. From the very commencement of the evening she had not once stirred from her seat; no one had thought of asking her to dance. One flaxen-headed youth of sixteen had, through lack of a partner, been on the point of addressing this lady, and had taken a step in her direction, but had thought better of it, stared at her, and hurriedly dived into the crowd. You can fancy with what joyful amazement she agreed to my proposal! I led her in triumph right across the ballroom, picked out two chairs, and sat down with her in the ring of the mazurka, among ten couples, almost opposite the prince, who had, of course, been offered the first place. The prince, as I have said already, was dancing with Liza. Neither I nor my partner was disturbed by invitations; consequently, we had plenty of time for conversation. To tell the truth, my partner was not conspicuous for her capacity for the utterance of words in consecutive speech; she used her mouth principally for the achievement of a strange downward smile such as I had never till then beheld; while she raised her eyes upward, as though some unseen force were pulling her face in two. But I did not feel her lack of eloquence. Happily I felt full of wrath, and my partner did not make me shy. I fell to finding fault with everything and every one in the world, with especial emphasis on town-bred youngsters and Petersburg dandies; and went to such lengths at last, that my partner gradually ceased smiling, and instead of turning her eyes upward, began suddenly—from astonishment, I suppose—to squint, and that so strangely, as though she had for the first time observed the fact that she had a nose on her face. And one of the lions, referred to above, who was sitting next me, did not once take his eyes off me; he positively turned to me with the expression of an actor on the stage, who has waked up in an unfamiliar place, as though he would say, 'Is it really you!' While I poured forth this tirade, I still, however, kept watch on the prince and Liza. They were continually invited; but I suffered less when they were both dancing; and even when they were sitting side by side, and smiling as they talked to each other that sweet smile which hardly leaves the faces of happy lovers, even then I was not in such torture; but when Liza flitted across the room with some desperate dandy of an hussar, while the prince with her blue gauze scarf on his knees followed her dreamily with his eyes, as though delighting in his conquest;—then, oh! then, I went through intolerable agonies, and in my anger gave vent to such spiteful observations, that the pupils of my partner's eyes simply fastened on her nose! Meanwhile the mazurka was drawing to a close. They were beginning the figure called *la confidente*. In this figure the lady sits in the middle of a circle, chooses another lady as her confidant, and whispers in her ear the name of the gentleman with whom she wishes to dance. Her partner conducts one after another of the dancers to her; but the lady, who is in the secret, refuses them, till at last the happy man fixed on beforehand arrives. Liza sat in the middle of the circle and chose the daughter of the host, one of those young ladies of whom one says, 'God help them!' . . . The prince proceeded to discover her choice. After presenting about a dozen young men to her in vain (the daughter of the house refused them all with the most amiable of smiles), he at last turned to me. Something extraordinary took place within me at that instant; I, as it were, twitched all over, and would have refused, but got up and went along. The prince conducted me to Liza. . . . She did not even look at me; the daughter of the house shook her head in refusal, the prince turned to me, and, probably incited by the goose-like expression of my face, made me a deep bow. This sarcastic bow, this refusal, transmitted to me through my triumphant rival, his careless smile, Liza's indifferent inattention, all this lashed me to frenzy. . . . I moved up to the prince and whispered furiously, 'You think fit to laugh at me, it seems?'

The prince looked at me with contemptuous surprise, took my arm again, and making a show of re-conducting me to my seat, answered coldly, 'I?'

'Yes, you!' I went on in a whisper, obeying, however—that is to say, following him to my place; 'you; but I do not intend to permit any empty-headed Petersburg upstart——'

The prince smiled tranquilly, almost condescendingly, pressed my arm, whispered, 'I understand you; but this is not the place; we will have a word later,' turned away from me, went up to Bizmyonkov, and led him up to Liza. The pale little official turned out to be the chosen partner. Liza got up to meet him.

Sitting beside my partner with the dejected beetle on her head, I felt almost a hero. My heart beat violently, my breast heaved gallantly under my starched shirt front, I drew deep and hurried breaths, and suddenly gave the local lion near me such a magnificent glare that there was an involuntary quiver of his foot in my direction. Having disposed of this person, I scanned the whole circle of dancers. . . . I fancied two or three gentlemen were staring at me with some perplexity; but, in general, my conversation with the prince had passed unnoticed. . . . My rival was already back in his chair, perfectly composed, and with the same smile on his face. Bizmyonkov led Liza back to her place. She gave him a friendly bow, and at once turned to the prince, as I fancied, with some alarm. But he laughed in response, with a graceful wave of his hand, and must have said something very agreeable to her, for she flushed with delight, dropped her eyes, and then bent them with affectionate reproach upon him.

The heroic frame of mind, which had suddenly developed in me, had not disappeared by the end of the mazurka; but I did not indulge in any more epigrams or 'quizzing.' I contented myself with glancing occasionally with gloomy severity at my partner, who was obviously beginning to be afraid of me, and was utterly tongue-tied and continuously blinking by the time I placed her under the protection of her mother, a very fat woman with a red cap on her head. Having consigned the scared maiden lady to her natural belongings, I turned away to a window, folded my arms, and began to await what would happen. I had rather long to wait. The prince was the whole time surrounded by his host—surrounded, simply, as England is surrounded by the sea,—to say nothing of the other members of the marshal's family and the rest of the guests. And besides, he could hardly go up to such an insignificant person as me and begin to talk without arousing a general feeling of surprise. This insignificance, I remember, was positively a joy to me at the time. 'All right,' I thought, as I watched him courteously addressing first one and then another highly respected personage, honoured by his notice, if only for an 'instant's flash,' as the poets say;—'all right, my dear . . . you'll come to me soon—I've insulted you, anyway.' At last the prince, adroitly escaping from the throng of his adorers, passed close by me, looked somewhere between the window and my hair, was turning away, and suddenly stood still, as though he had recollected something. 'Ah, yes!' he said, turning to me with a smile, 'by the way, I have a little matter to talk to you about.'

Two country gentlemen, of the most persistent, who were obstinately pursuing the prince, probably imagined the 'little matter' to relate to official business, and respectfully fell back. The prince took my arm and led me apart. My heart was thumping at my ribs.

'You, I believe,' he began, emphasising the word *you*, and looking at my chin with a contemptuous expression, which, strange to say, was supremely becoming to his fresh and handsome face, 'you said something abusive to me?'

'I said what I thought,' I replied, raising my voice.

'Sh . . . quietly,' he observed; 'decent people don't bawl. You would like, perhaps, to fight me?'

'That's your affair,' I answered, drawing myself up.

'I shall be obliged to challenge you,' he remarked carelessly, 'if you don't withdraw your expressions. . . .'

'I do not intend to withdraw from anything,' I rejoined with pride.

'Really?' he observed, with an ironical smile. 'In that case,' he continued, after a brief pause, 'I shall have the honour of sending my second to you to-morrow.'

'Very good,' I said in a voice, if possible, even more indifferent.

The prince gave a slight bow.

'I cannot prevent you from considering me empty-headed,' he added, with a haughty droop of his eyelids; 'but the Princes N—— cannot be upstarts. Good-bye till we meet, Mr. . . . Mr. Shtukaturin.'

He quickly turned his back on me, and again approached his host, who was already beginning to get excited.

Mr. Shtukaturin! . . . My name is Tchulkaturin. . . . I could think of nothing to say to him in reply to this last insult, and could only gaze after him with fury. 'Till to-morrow,' I muttered, clenching my teeth, and I at once looked for an officer of my acquaintance, a cavalry captain in the Uhlans, called Koloberdyaev, a desperate rake, and a very good fellow. To him I related, in few words, my quarrel with the prince, and asked him to be my second. He, of course, promptly consented, and I went home.

I could not sleep all night—from excitement, not from cowardice. I am not a coward. I positively thought very little of the possibility confronting me of losing my life—that, as the Germans assure us, highest good on earth. I could think only of Liza, of my ruined hopes, of what I ought to do. 'Ought I to try to kill the prince?' I asked myself; and, of course, I wanted to kill him—not from revenge, but from a desire for Liza's good. 'But she will not survive such a blow,' I went on. 'No, better let him kill me!' I must own it was an agreeable reflection, too, that I, an obscure provincial person, had forced a man of such consequence to fight a duel with me.

The morning light found me still absorbed in these reflections; and, not long after it, appeared Koloberdyaev.

'Well,' he asked me, entering my room with a clatter, 'where's the prince's second?'

'Upon my word,' I answered with annoyance, 'it's seven o'clock at the most; the prince is still asleep, I should imagine.'

'In that case,' replied the cavalry officer, in nowise daunted, 'order some tea for me. My head aches from yesterday evening. . . . I've not taken my clothes off all night. Though, indeed,' he added with a yawn, 'I don't as a rule often take my clothes off.'

Some tea was given him. He drank off six glasses of tea and rum, smoked four pipes, told me he had on the previous day bought, for next to nothing, a horse the coachman refused to drive, and that he was meaning to drive her out with one of her fore legs tied up, and fell asleep, without undressing, on the sofa, with a pipe in his mouth. I got up and put my papers to rights. One note of invitation from Liza, the one note I had received from her, I was on the point of putting in my bosom, but on second thoughts I flung it in a drawer. Koloberdyaev was snoring feebly, with his head hanging from the leather pillow. . . . For a long while, I remember, I scrutinised his unkempt, daring, careless, and good-natured face. At ten o'clock the man announced the arrival of Bizmyonkov. The prince had chosen him as second.

We both together roused the soundly sleeping cavalry officer. He sat up, stared at us with dim eyes, in a hoarse voice demanded vodka. He recovered himself, and exchanging greetings with Bizmyonkov, he went with him into the next room to arrange matters. The consultation of the worthy seconds did not last long. A quarter of an hour later, they both came into my bedroom. Koloberdyaev announced to me that 'we're going to fight to-day at three o'clock with pistols.' In silence I bent my head, in token of my agreement. Bizmyonkov at once took leave of us, and departed. He was rather pale and inwardly agitated, like a man unused to such jobs, but he was, nevertheless, very polite and chilly. I felt, as it were, conscience-stricken in his presence, and did not dare look him in the face.

Koloberdyaev began telling me about his horse. This conversation was very welcome to me. I was afraid he would mention Liza. But the good-natured cavalry officer was not a gossip, and, moreover, he despised all women, calling them, God knows why, green stuff. At two o'clock we had lunch, and at three we were at the place fixed upon — the very birch copse in which I had once walked with Liza, a couple of yards from the precipice.

We arrived first; but the prince and Bizmyonkov did not keep us long waiting. The prince was, without exaggeration, as fresh as a rose; his brown eyes looked out with excessive cordiality from under the peak of his cap. He was smoking a cigar, and on seeing Koloberdyaev shook his hand in a friendly way. Even to me he bowed very genially. I was conscious, on the contrary, of being pale, and my hands, to my terrible vexation, were slightly trembling . . . my throat was parched. . . . I had never fought a duel before. 'O God!' I thought; 'if only that ironical gentleman doesn't take my agitation for timidity!' I was inwardly cursing my nerves; but glancing, at last, straight in the prince's face, and catching on his lips an almost imperceptible smile, I suddenly felt furious again, and was at once at my ease. Meanwhile, our seconds were fixing the barrier, measuring out the paces, loading the pistols. Koloberdyaev did most; Bizmyonkov rather watched him. It was a magnificent day — as fine as the day of that ever-memorable walk. The thick blue of the sky peeped, as then, through the golden green of the leaves. Their lisping seemed to mock me. The prince went on smoking his cigar, leaning with his shoulder against the trunk of a young lime-tree. . . .

'Kindly take your places, gentlemen; ready,' Koloberdyaev pronounced at last, handing us pistols.

The prince walked a few steps away, stood still, and, turning his head, asked me over his shoulder, 'You still refuse to take back your words, then?'

I tried to answer him; but my voice failed me, and I had to content myself with a contemptuous wave of the hand. The prince smiled again, and took up his position in his place. We began to approach one another. I raised my pistol, was about to aim at my enemy's chest — but suddenly tilted it up, as though some one had given my elbow a shove, and fired. The prince tottered, and put his left hand to his left temple — a thread of blood was flowing down his cheek from under the white leather glove. Bizmyonkov rushed up to him.

'It's all right,' he said, taking off his cap, which the bullet had pierced; 'since it's in the head, and I've not fallen, it must be a mere scratch.'

He calmly pulled a cambric handkerchief out of his pocket, and put it to his blood-stained curls.

I stared at him, as though I were turned to stone, and did not stir.

'Go up to the barrier, if you please!' Koloberdyaev observed severely.

I obeyed.

'Is the duel to go on?' he added, addressing Bizmyonkov.

Bizmyonkov made him no answer. But the prince, without taking the handkerchief from the wound, without even giving himself the satisfaction of tormenting me at the barrier, replied with a smile, 'The duel is at an end,' and fired into the air. I was almost crying with rage and vexation. This man by his magnanimity had utterly trampled me in the mud; he had completely crushed me. I was on the point of making objections, on the point of demanding that he should fire at me. But he came up to me, and held out his hand.

'It's all forgotten between us, isn't it?' he said in a friendly voice.

I looked at his blanched face, at the blood-stained handkerchief, and utterly confounded, put to shame, and annihilated, I pressed his hand.

'Gentlemen!' he added, turning to the seconds, 'everything, I hope, will be kept secret?'

'Of course!' cried Koloberdyaev; 'but, prince, allow me . . .'

And he himself bound up his head.

The prince, as he went away, bowed to me once more. But Bizmyonkov did not even glance at me. Shattered—morally shattered—I went homewards with Koloberdyaev.

'Why, what's the matter with you?' the cavalry captain asked me. 'Set your mind at rest; the wound's not serious. He'll be able to dance by tomorrow, if you like. Or are you sorry you didn't kill him? You're wrong, if you are; he's a first-rate fellow.'

'What business had he to spare me!' I muttered at last.

'Oh, so that's it!' the cavalry captain rejoined tranquilly. . . . 'Ugh, you writing fellows are too much for me!'

I don't know what put it into his head to consider me an author.

I absolutely decline to describe my torments during the evening following upon that luckless duel. My vanity suffered indescribably. It was not my conscience that tortured me; the consciousness of my imbecility crushed me. 'I have given myself the last decisive blow by my own act!' I kept repeating, as I strode up and down my room. 'The prince, wounded by me, and forgiving me. . . . Yes, Liza is now his. Now nothing can save her, nothing can hold her back on the edge of the abyss.' I knew very well that our duel could not be kept secret, in spite of the prince's words; in any case, it could not remain a secret for Liza.

'The prince is not such a fool,' I murmured in a frenzy of rage, 'as not to profit by it.' . . . But, meanwhile, I was mistaken. The whole town knew of the duel and of its real cause next day, of course. But the prince had not blabbed of it; on the contrary, when, with his head bandaged and an explanation ready, he made his appearance before Liza, she had already heard everything. . . . Whether Bizmyonkov had betrayed me, or the news had reached her by other channels, I cannot say. Though, indeed, can anything ever be concealed in a little town? You can fancy how Liza received him, how all the family of the Ozhogins received him! As for me, I suddenly became an object of universal indignation and loathing, a monster, a jealous bloodthirsty madman. My few acquaintances shunned me as if I were a leper. The authorities of the town promptly addressed the prince, with a proposal to punish me in a severe and befitting manner. Nothing but the persistent and urgent entreaties of the prince himself averted the calamity that menaced me. That man was fated to annihilate me in every way. By his generosity he had shut, as it were, a coffin-lid down upon me. It's needless to say that the Ozhogins' doors were at once closed against me. Kirilla Matveitch even sent me back a bit of pencil I had left in his house. In reality, he, of all people, had no reason to be angry with me. My 'insane' (that was the expression current in the town) jealousy had pointed out, defined, so to speak, the relations of the prince to Liza. Both the old Ozhogins themselves and their fellow-citizens began to look on him almost as betrothed to her. This could not, as a fact, have been quite to his liking. But he was greatly attracted by Liza; and meanwhile, he had not at that time attained his aims. With all the adroitness of a clever man of the world, he took advantage of his new position, and promptly entered, as they say, into the spirit of his new part. . . .

But I! . . . For myself, for my future, I renounced all hopes, at that time. When suffering reaches the point of making our whole being creak and groan, like an overloaded cart, it ought to cease to be ridiculous . . . but no! laughter not only accompanies tears to the end, to exhaustion, to the impossibility of shedding more — it even rings and echoes, where the tongue is dumb, and complaint itself is dead. . . . And so, as in the first place I don't intend to expose myself as ridiculous, even to myself, and secondly as I am fearfully tired, I will put off the continuation, and please God the conclusion, of my story till to-morrow. . . .

March 29. A slight frost; yesterday it was thawing.

Yesterday I had not the strength to go on with my diary; like Poprishtchin, I lay, for the most part, on my bed, and talked to Terentyevna. What a woman! Sixty years ago she lost her first betrothed from the plague, she has outlived all her children, she is inexcusably old, drinks tea to her heart's desire, is well fed, and warmly clothed; and what do you suppose she was talking to me about, all day yesterday? I had sent another utterly destitute old woman the collar of an old livery, half moth- eaten, to put on her vest (she wears strips over the chest by way of vest) . . . and why wasn't it given to her? 'But I'm your nurse; I should think . . . Oh . . . oh, my good sir, it's too bad of you . . . after I've looked after you as I have!' . . . and so on. The merciless old woman utterly wore me out with her reproaches. . . . But to get back to my story.

And so, I suffered like a dog, whose hindquarters have been run over by a wheel. It was only then, only after my banishment from the Ozhogins' house, that I fully realised how much happiness a man can extract from the contemplation of his own unhappiness. O men! pitiful race, indeed! . . . But, away with philosophical reflections. . . . I spent my days in complete solitude, and could only by the most roundabout and even humiliating methods find out what was passing in the Ozhogins' household, and what the prince was doing. My man had made friends with the cousin of the latter's coachman's wife. This acquaintance afforded me some slight relief, and my man soon guessed, from my hints and little presents, what he was to talk about to his master when he pulled his boots off every evening. Sometimes I chanced to meet some one of the Ozhogins' family, Bizmyonkov, or the prince in the street. . . . To the prince and to Bizmyonkov I bowed, but I did not enter into conversation with them. Liza I only saw three times: once, with her mamma, in a fashionable shop; once, in an open carriage with her father and mother and the prince; and once, in church. Of course, I was not impudent enough to approach her, and only watched her from a distance. In the shop she was very much preoccupied, but cheerful. . . . She was ordering something for herself, and busily matching ribbons. Her mother was gazing at her, with her hands folded on her lap, and her nose in the air, smiling with that foolish and devoted smile which is only permissible in adoring mothers. In the carriage with the prince, Liza was . . . I shall never forget that meeting! The old people were sitting in the back seats of the carriage, the prince and Liza in the front. She was paler than usual; on her cheek two patches of pink could just be seen. She was half facing the prince; leaning on her straight right arm (in the left hand she was holding a sunshade), with her little head drooping languidly, she was looking straight into his face with her expressive eyes. At that instant she surrendered herself utterly to him, intrusted herself to him for ever. I had not time to get a good look at his face—the carriage galloped by too quickly,—but I fancied that he too was deeply touched.

The third time I saw her in church. Not more than ten days had passed since the day when I met her in the carriage with the prince, not more than three weeks since the day of my duel. The business upon which the prince had come to O—— was by now completed. But he still kept putting off his departure. At Petersburg, he was reported to be ill. In the town, it was expected every day that he would make a proposal in form to Kirilla Matveitch. I was myself only awaiting this final blow to go away for ever. The town of O—— had grown hateful to me. I could not stay indoors, and wandered from morning to night about the suburbs. One grey, gloomy day, as I was coming back from a walk, which had been cut short by the rain, I went into a church. The evening service had only just begun, there were very few people; I looked round me, and suddenly, near a window, caught sight of a familiar profile. For the first instant, I did not recognise it: that pale face, that spiritless glance, those sunken cheeks—could it be the same Liza I had seen a fortnight before? Wrapped in a cloak, without a hat on, with the cold light from the broad white window falling on her from one side, she was gazing fixedly at the holy image, and seemed striving to pray, striving to awake from a sort of listless stupor. A red-cheeked, fat little page with yellow trimmings on his chest was standing behind her, and, with his hands clasped behind his back, stared in sleepy bewilderment at his mistress. I trembled all over, was about to go up to her, but stopped short. I felt choked by a torturing presentiment. Till the very end of the evening service, Liza did not stir. All the people went out, a beadle began sweeping out the church, but still she did not move from her place. The page went up to her, said something to her, touched her dress; she looked round, passed her hand over her face, and went away. I followed her home at a little distance, and then returned to my lodging.

'She is lost!' I cried, when I had got into my room.

As a man, I don't know to this day what my sensations were at that moment. I flung myself, I remember, with clasped hands, on the sofa and fixed my eyes on the floor. But I don't know—in the midst of my woe I was, as it were, pleased at something. . . . I would not admit this for anything in the world, if I were not writing only for myself. . . . I had been tormented, certainly, by terrible, harassing suspicions . . . and who knows, I should, perhaps, have been greatly disconcerted if they had not been fulfilled. 'Such is the heart of man!' some middle-aged Russian teacher would exclaim at this point in an expressive voice, while he raises a fat forefinger, adorned with a cornelian ring. But what have we to do with the opinion of a Russian teacher, with an expressive voice and a cornelian on his finger?

Be that as it may, my presentiment turned out to be well founded. Suddenly the news was all over the town that the prince had gone away, presumably in consequence of a summons from Petersburg; that he had gone away without making any proposal to Kirilla Matveitch or his wife, and that Liza would have to deplore his treachery till the end of her days. The prince's departure was utterly unexpected, for only the evening before his coachman, so my man assured me, had not the slightest suspicion of his master's intentions. This piece of news threw me into a perfect fever. I at once dressed, and was on the point of hastening to the Ozhogins', but on thinking the matter over I considered it more seemly to wait till the next day. I lost nothing, however, by remaining at home. The same evening, there came to see me in all haste a certain Pandopipopulo, a wandering Greek, stranded by some chance in the town of O——, a scandalmonger of the first magnitude, who had been more indignant with me than any one for my duel with the prince. He did not even give my man time to announce him; he fairly burst into my room, warmly pressed my hand, begged my pardon a thousand times, called me a paragon of magnanimity and courage, painted the prince in the darkest colours, censured the old Ozhogins, who, in his opinion, had been punished as they deserved, made a slighting reference to Liza in passing, and hurried off again, kissing me on my shoulder. Among other things, I learned from him that the prince, *en vrai grand seigneur,*[1] on the eve of his departure, in response to a delicate hint from Kirilla Matveitch, had answered coldly that he had no intention of deceiving any one, and no idea of marrying, had risen, made his bow, and that was all. . . .

Next day I set off to the Ozhogins'. The shortsighted footman leaped up from his bench on my appearance, with the rapidity of lightning. I bade him announce me; the footman hurried away and returned at once. 'Walk in,' he said; 'you are begged to go in.' I went into Kirilla Matveitch's study. . . . The rest to-morrow.

March 30. *Frost.*

And so I went into Kirilla Matveitch's study. I would pay any one handsomely, who could show me now my own face at the moment when that highly respected official, hurriedly flinging together his dressing-gown, approached me with outstretched arms. I must have been a perfect picture of modest triumph, indulgent sympathy, and boundless magnanimity. . . . I felt myself something in the style of Scipio Africanus. Ozhogin was visibly confused and cast down, he avoided my eyes, and kept fidgeting about. I noticed, too, that he spoke unnaturally loudly, and in general expressed himself very vaguely. Vaguely, but with warmth, he begged my forgiveness, vaguely alluded to their departed guest, added a few vague generalities about deception and the instability of earthly blessings, and, suddenly feeling the tears in his eyes, hastened to take a pinch of snuff, probably in order to deceive me as to the cause of his tearfulness. . . . He used the Russian green snuff, and it's well known that that article forces even old men to shed tears that make the human eye look dull and senseless for several minutes.

I behaved, of course, very cautiously with the old man, inquired after the health of his wife and daughter, and at once artfully turned the conversation on to the interesting subject of the rotation of crops. I was dressed as usual, but the feeling of gentle propriety and soft indulgence which filled me gave me a fresh and festive sensation, as though I had on a white waistcoat and a white cravat. One thing agitated me, the thought of seeing

[1] *en vrai grand seigneur*] in a truly lordly manner.

Liza. . . . Ozhogin, at last, proposed of his own accord to take me up to his wife. The kind-hearted but foolish woman was at first terribly embarrassed on seeing me; but her brain was not capable of retaining the same impression for long, and so she was soon at her ease. At last I saw Liza . . . she came into the room. . . .

I had expected to find in her a shamed and penitent sinner, and had assumed beforehand the most affectionate and reassuring expression of face. . . . Why lie about it? I really loved her and was thirsting for the happiness of forgiving her, of holding out a hand to her; but to my unutterable astonishment, in response to my significant bow, she laughed coldly, observed carelessly, 'Oh, is that you?' and at once turned away from me. It is true that her laugh struck me as forced, and in any case did not accord well with her terribly thin face . . . but, all the same, I had not expected such a reception. . . . I looked at her with amazement . . . what a change had taken place in her! Between the child she had been and the woman before me, there was nothing in common. She had, as it were, grown up, straightened out; all the features of her face, especially her lips, seemed defined . . . her gaze had grown deeper, harder, and gloomier. I stayed on at the Ozhogins' till dinner-time. She got up, went out of the room, and came back again, answered questions with composure, and designedly took no notice of me. She wanted, I saw, to make me feel that I was not worth her anger, though I had been within an ace of killing her lover. I lost patience at last; a malicious allusion broke from my lips. . . . She started, glanced swiftly at me, got up, and going to the window, pronounced in a rather shaky voice, 'You can say anything you like, but let me tell you that I love that man, and always shall love him, and do not consider that he has done me any injury, quite the contrary.' . . . Her voice broke, she stopped . . . tried to control herself, but could not, burst into tears, and went out of the room. . . . The old people were much upset. . . . I pressed the hands of both, sighed, turned my eyes heavenward, and withdrew.

I am too weak, I have too little time left, I am not capable of describing in the same detail the new range of torturing reflections, firm resolutions, and all the other fruits of what is called inward conflict, that arose within me after the renewal of my acquaintance with the Ozhogins. I did not doubt that Liza still loved, and would long love, the prince . . . but as one reconciled to the inevitable, and anxious myself to conciliate, I did not even dream of her love. I desired only her affection, I desired to gain her confidence, her respect, which, we are assured by persons of experience, forms the surest basis for happiness in marriage. . . . Unluckily, I lost sight of one rather important circumstance, which was that Liza had hated me ever since the day of the duel. I found this out too late. I began, as before, to be a frequent visitor at the house of the Ozhogins. Kirilla Matveitch received me with more effusiveness and affability than he had ever done. I have even ground for believing that he would at that time have cheerfully given me his daughter, though I was certainly not a match to be coveted. Public opinion was very severe upon him and Liza, while, on the other hand, it extolled me to the skies. Liza's attitude to me was unchanged. She was, for the most part, silent; obeyed, when they begged her to eat, showed no outward signs of sorrow, but, for all that, was wasting away like a candle. I must do Kirilla Matveitch the justice to say that he spared her in every way. Old Madame Ozhogin only ruffled up her feathers like a hen, as she looked at her poor nestling. There was only one person Liza did not shun, though she did not talk much even to him, and that was Bizmyonkov. The old people were rather short, not to say rude, in their behaviour to him. They could not forgive him for having been second in the duel. But he went on going to see them, as though he did not notice their unamiability. With me he was very chilly, and — strange to say — I felt, as it were, afraid of him. This state of things went on for a fortnight. At last, after a sleepless night, I resolved to have it out with Liza, to open my heart to her, to tell her that, in spite of the past, in spite of all possible gossip and scandal, I should consider myself only too happy if she would give me her hand, and restore me her confidence. I really did seriously imagine that I was showing what they call in the school reading-books an unparalleled example of magnanimity, and that, from sheer amazement alone, she would consent. In any case, I resolved to have an explanation and to escape, at last, from suspense.

Behind the Ozhogins' house was a rather large garden, which ended in a little grove of lime-trees, neglected and overgrown. In the middle of this thicket stood an old summer-house in the Chinese style: a wooden paling separated the garden from a blind alley. Liza would sometimes walk, for hours together, alone in this garden. Kirilla Matveitch was aware of this, and forbade her being disturbed or followed; let her grief wear itself out, he said. When she could not be found indoors, they had only to ring a bell on the steps at dinner-time and she made her appearance at once, with the same stubborn silence on her lips and in her eyes, and some little leaf crushed up in her hand. So, noticing one day that she was not in the house, I made a show of going away, took leave of Kirilla Matveitch, put on my hat, and went out from the hall into the courtyard, and from the courtyard into the street, but promptly darted in at the gate again with extraordinary rapidity and hurried past the kitchen into the garden. Luckily no one noticed me. Without losing time in deliberation, I went with rapid steps into the grove. In a little path before me was standing Liza. My heart beat violently. I stood still, drew a deep sigh, and was just on the point of going up to her, when suddenly she lifted her hand without turning round, and began listening. . . . From behind the trees, in the direction of the blind alley, came a distinct sound of two knocks, as though some one were tapping at the paling. Liza clapped her hands together, there was heard the faint creak of the gate, and out of the thicket stepped Bizmyonkov. I hastily hid behind a tree. Liza turned towards him without speaking. . . . Without speaking, he drew her arm in his, and the two walked slowly along the path together. I looked after them in amazement. They stopped, looked round, disappeared behind the bushes, reappeared again, and finally went into the summer-house. This summer-house was a diminutive round edifice, with a door and one little window. In the middle stood an old one-legged table, overgrown with fine green moss; two discoloured deal benches stood along the sides, some distance from the damp and darkened walls. Here, on exceptionally hot days, in bygone times, perhaps once a year or so, they had drunk tea. The door did not quite shut, the window-frame had long ago come out of the window, and hung disconsolately, only attached at one corner, like a bird's broken wing. I stole up to the summer-house, and peeped cautiously through the chink in the window. Liza was sitting on one of the benches, with her head drooping. Her right hand lay on her knees, the left Bizmyonkov was holding in both his hands. He was looking sympathetically at her.

'How do you feel to-day?' he asked her in a low voice.

'Just the same,' she answered, 'not better, nor worse.—The emptiness, the fearful emptiness!' she added, raising her eyes dejectedly.

Bizmyonkov made her no answer.

'What do you think,' she went on: 'will he write to me once more?'

'I don't think so, Lizaveta Kirillovna!'

She was silent.

'And after all, why should he write? He told me everything in his first letter. I could not be his wife; but I have been happy . . . not for long . . . I have been happy . . .'

Bizmyonkov looked down.

'Ah,' she went on quickly, 'if you knew how I loathe that Tchulkaturin . . . I always fancy I see on that man's hands . . . his blood.' (I shuddered behind my chink.) 'Though indeed,' she added, dreamily, 'who knows, perhaps, if it had not been for that duel. . . . Ah, when I saw him wounded I felt at once that I was altogether his.'

'Tchulkaturin loves you,' observed Bizmyonkov.

'What is that to me? I don't want any one's love.' . . . She stopped and added slowly, 'Except yours. Yes, my friend, your love is necessary to me; except for you, I should be lost. You have helped me to bear terrible moments . . .'

She broke off . . . Bizmyonkov began with fatherly tenderness stroking her hand.

'There's no help for it! What is one to do! what is one to do, Lizaveta Kirillovna!' he repeated several times.

'And now indeed,' she went on in a lifeless voice, 'I should die, I think, if it were not for you. It's you alone that keep me up; besides, you remind me of him. . . . You knew all about it, you see. Do you remember how fine he was that day. . . . But forgive me; it must be hard for you. . . .'

'Go on, go on! Nonsense! Bless you!' Bizmyonkov interrupted her.

She pressed his hand.

'You are very good, Bizmyonkov,' she went on; 'you are good as an angel. What can I do! I feel I shall love him to the grave. I have forgiven him, I am grateful to him. God give him happiness! May God give him a wife after his own heart'—and her eyes filled with tears—'if only he does not forget me, if only he will sometimes think of his Liza!—Let us go,' she added, after a brief silence.

Bizmyonkov raised her hand to his lips.

'I know,' she began again hotly, 'every one is blaming me now, every one is throwing stones at me. Let them! I wouldn't, any way, change my misery for their happiness . . . no! no! . . . He did not love me for long, but he loved me! He never deceived me, he never told me I should be his wife; I never dreamed of it myself. It was only poor papa hoped for it. And even now I am not altogether unhappy; the memory remains to me, and however fearful the results . . . I'm stifling here . . . it was here I saw him the last time. . . . Let's go into the air.'

They got up. I had only just time to skip on one side and hide behind a thick lime-tree. They came out of the summer-house, and, as far as I could judge by the sound of their steps, went away into the thicket. I don't know how long I went on standing there, without stirring from my place, plunged in a sort of senseless amazement, when suddenly I heard steps again. I started, and peeped cautiously out from my hiding-place. Bizmyonkov and Liza were coming back along the same path. Both were greatly agitated, especially Bizmyonkov. I fancied he was crying. Liza stopped, looked at him, and distinctly uttered the following words: 'I do consent, Bizmyonkov. I would never have agreed if you were only trying to save me, to rescue me from a terrible position, but you love me, you know everything—and you love me. I shall never find a trustier, truer friend. I will be your wife.'

Bizmyonkov kissed her hand: she smiled at him mournfully and moved away towards the house. Bizmyonkov rushed into the thicket, and I went my way. Seeing that Bizmyonkov had apparently said to Liza precisely what I had intended to say to her, and she had given him precisely the reply I was longing to hear from her, there was no need for me to trouble myself further. Within a fortnight she was married to him. The old Ozhogins were thankful to get any husband for her.

Now, tell me, am I not a superfluous man? Didn't I play throughout the whole story the part of a superfluous person? The prince's part . . . of that it's needless to speak; Bizmyonkov's part, too, is comprehensible. . . . But I—with what object was I mixed up in it? . . . A senseless fifth wheel to the cart! . . . Ah, it's bitter, bitter for me! . . . But there, as the barge-haulers say, 'One more pull, and one more yet,'—one day more, and one more yet, and there will be no more bitter nor sweet for me.

March 31.

I'm in a bad way. I am writing these lines in bed. Since yesterday evening there has been a sudden change in the weather. To-day is hot, almost a summer day. Everything is thawing, breaking up, flowing away. The air is full of the smell of the opened earth, a strong, heavy, stifling smell. Steam is rising on all sides. The sun seems beating, seems smiting everything to pieces. I am very ill, I feel that I am breaking up.

I meant to write my diary, and, instead of that, what have I done? I have related one incident of my life. I gossiped on, slumbering reminiscences were awakened and drew me away. I have written, without haste, in detail, as though I had years before me. And here now, there's no time to go on. Death, death is coming. I can hear her menacing *crescendo*. The time is come . . . the time is come! . . .

And indeed, what does it matter? Isn't it all the same whatever I write? In sight of death the last earthly cares vanish. I feel I have grown calm; I am becoming simpler, clearer. Too late I've gained sense! . . . It's a strange thing! I have grown calm—certainly, and at the same time . . . I'm full of dread. Yes, I'm full of dread. Half hanging over the silent, yawning abyss, I shudder, turn away, with greedy intentness gaze at everything about me. Every object is doubly precious to me. I cannot gaze enough at my poor, cheerless room, saying farewell to each spot on my walls. Take your fill for the last time, my eyes. Life is retreating; slowly and smoothly she is flying away from me, as the shore flies from the eyes of one at sea. The old yellow face of my nurse, tied up in a dark kerchief, the hissing samovar on the table, the pot of geranium in the window, and you, my poor dog, Tresór, the pen I write these lines with, my own hand, I see you now . . . here you are, here. . . . Is it possible . . . can it be, to-day . . . I shall never see you again! It's hard for a live creature to part with life! Why do you fawn on me, poor dog? why do you come putting your forepaws on the bed, with your stump of a tail wagging so violently, and your kind, mournful eyes fixed on me all the while? Are you sorry for me? or do you feel already that your master will soon be gone? Ah, if I could only keep my thoughts, too, resting on all the objects in my room! I know these reminiscences are dismal and of no importance, but I have no other. 'The emptiness, the fearful emptiness!' as Liza said.

O my God, my God! Here I am dying. . . . A heart capable of loving and ready to love will soon cease to beat. . . . And can it be it will be still for ever without having once known happiness, without having once expanded under the sweet burden of bliss? Alas! it's impossible, impossible, I know. . . . If only now, at least, before death — for death after all is a sacred thing, after all it elevates any being — if any kind, sad, friendly voice would sing over me a farewell song of my own sorrow, I could, perhaps, be resigned to it. But to die stupidly, stupidly. . . .

I believe I'm beginning to rave.

Farewell, life! farewell, my garden! and you, my lime-trees! When the summer comes, do not forget to be clothed with flowers from head to foot . . . and may it be sweet for people to lie in your fragrant shade, on the fresh grass, among the whispering chatter of your leaves, lightly stirred by the wind. Farewell, farewell! Farewell, everything and for ever!

Farewell, Liza! I wrote those two words, and almost laughed aloud. This exclamation strikes me as taken out of a book. It's as though I were writing a sentimental novel and ending up a despairing letter. . . .

To-morrow is the first of April. Can I be going to die to-morrow? That would be really too unseemly. It's just right for me, though . . .

How the doctor did chatter to-day!

April 1.

It is over. . . . Life is over. I shall certainly die to-day. It's hot outside . . . almost suffocating . . . or is it that my lungs are already refusing to breathe? My little comedy is played out. The curtain is falling.

Sinking into nothing, I cease to be superfluous . . .

Ah, how brilliant that sun is! Those mighty beams breathe of eternity . . .

Farewell, Terentyevna! . . . This morning as she sat at the window she was crying . . . perhaps over me . . . and perhaps because she too will soon have to die. I have made her promise not to kill Tresór.

It's hard for me to write. . . . I will put down the pen. . . . It's high time; death is already approaching with ever-increasing rumble, like a carriage at night over the pavement; it is here, it is flitting about me, like the light breath which made the prophet's hair stand up on end.

I am dying. . . . Live, you who are living,

'And about the grave
May youthful life rejoice,
And nature heedless
Glow with eternal beauty.'

Note by the Editor. — Under this last line was a head in profile with a big streak of hair and moustaches, with eyes *en face*,[1] and eyelashes like rays; and under the head some one had written the following words:

[1] *en face*] in front.

'This manuscript was read
And the Contents of it Not Approved
By Peter Zudotyeshin
My My My
My dear Sir,
Peter Zudotyeshin,
Dear Sir.'

But as the handwriting of these lines was not in the least like the handwriting in which the other part of the manuscript was written, the editor considers that he is justified in concluding that the above lines were added subsequently by another person, especially since it has come to his (the editor's) knowledge that Mr. Tchulkaturin actually did die on the night between the 1st and 2nd of April in the year 18—, at his native place, Sheep's Springs.

First Love

THE party had long ago broken up. The clock struck half-past twelve. There was left in the room only the master of the house and Sergei Nikolaevitch and Vladimir Petrovitch.

The master of the house rang and ordered the remains of the supper to be cleared away. 'And so it's settled,' he observed, sitting back farther in his easy-chair and lighting a cigar; 'each of us is to tell the story of his first love. It's your turn, Sergei Nikolaevitch.'

Sergei Nikolaevitch, a round little man with a plump, light-complexioned face, gazed first at the master of the house, then raised his eyes to the ceiling. 'I had no first love,' he said at last; 'I began with the second.'

'How was that?'

'It's very simple. I was eighteen when I had my first flirtation with a charming young lady, but I courted her just as though it were nothing new to me; just as I courted others later on. To speak accurately, the first and last time I was in love was with my nurse when I was six years old; but that's in the remote past. The details of our relations have slipped out of my memory, and even if I remembered them, whom could they interest?'

'Then how's it to be?' began the master of the house. 'There was nothing much of interest about my first love either; I never fell in love with any one till I met Anna Nikolaevna, now my wife,—and everything went as smoothly as possible with us; our parents arranged the match, we were very soon in love with each other, and got married without loss of time. My story can be told in a couple of words. I must confess, gentlemen, in bringing up the subject of first love, I reckoned upon you, I won't say old, but no longer young, bachelors. Can't you enliven us with something, Vladimir Petrovitch?'

'My first love, certainly, was not quite an ordinary one,' responded, with some reluctance, Vladimir Petrovitch, a man of forty, with black hair turning grey.

'Ah!' said the master of the house and Sergei Nikolaevitch with one voice: 'So much the better. . . . Tell us about it.'

'If you wish it . . . or no; I won't tell the story; I'm no hand at telling a story; I make it dry and brief, or spun out and affected. If you'll allow me, I'll write out all I remember and read it you.'

His friends at first would not agree, but Vladimir Petrovitch insisted on his own way. A fortnight later they were together again, and Vladimir Petrovitch kept his word.

His manuscript contained the following story: —

I

I WAS sixteen then. It happened in the summer of 1833.

I lived in Moscow with my parents. They had taken a country house for the summer near the Kalouga gate, facing the Neskutchny gardens. I was preparing for the university, but did not work much and was in no hurry.

No one interfered with my freedom. I did what I liked, especially after parting with my last tutor, a Frenchman who had never been able to get used to the idea that he had fallen 'like a bomb' (*comme une bombe*) into Russia, and would lie sluggishly in bed with an expression of exasperation on his face for days together. My father treated me with careless kindness; my mother scarcely noticed me, though she had no children except me; other cares completely absorbed her. My father, a man still young and very handsome, had married her from mercenary considerations; she was ten years older than he. My mother led a melancholy life; she was for ever agitated, jealous and angry, but not in my father's presence; she was very much afraid of him, and he was severe, cold, and distant in his behaviour. . . . I have never seen a man more elaborately serene, self-confident, and commanding.

I shall never forget the first weeks I spent at the country house. The weather was magnificent; we left town on the 9th of May, on St. Nicholas's day. I used to walk about in our garden, in the Neskutchny gardens, and beyond the town gates; I would take some book with me — Keidanov's Course, for instance — but I rarely looked into it, and more often than anything declaimed verses aloud; I knew a great deal of poetry by heart; my blood was in a ferment and my heart ached — so sweetly and absurdly; I was all hope and anticipation, was a little frightened of something, and full of wonder at everything, and was on the tiptoe of expectation; my imagination played continually, fluttering rapidly about the same fancies, like martins about a bell-tower at dawn; I dreamed, was sad, even wept; but through the tears and through the sadness, inspired by a musical verse, or the beauty of evening, shot up like grass in spring the delicious sense of youth and effervescent life.

I had a horse to ride; I used to saddle it myself and set off alone for long rides, break into a rapid gallop and fancy myself a knight at a tournament. How gaily the wind whistled in my ears! or turning my face towards the sky,

I would absorb its shining radiance and blue into m
to welcome it.

I remember that at that time the image of woma
scarcely ever arose in definite shape in my brain; but i
felt, lay hidden a half-conscious, shamefaced present
new, unutterably sweet, feminine. . . .

This presentiment, this expectation, permeated m being; I breathed in it, it coursed through my veins with every drop of blood . . . it was destined to be soon fulfilled.

The place, where we settled for the summer, consisted of a wooden manor-house with columns and two small lodges; in the lodge on the left there was a tiny factory for the manufacture of cheap wall-papers. . . . I had more than once strolled that way to look at about a dozen thin and dishevelled boys with greasy smocks and worn faces, who were perpetually jumping on to wooden levers, that pressed down the square blocks of the press, and so by the weight of their feeble bodies struck off the variegated patterns of the wall-papers. The lodge on the right stood empty, and was to let. One day—three weeks after the 9th of May—the blinds in the windows of this lodge were drawn up, women's faces appeared at them—some family had installed themselves in it. I remember the same day at dinner, my mother inquired of the butler who were our new neighbours, and hearing the name of the Princess Zasyekin, first observed with some respect, 'Ah! a princess!' . . . and then added, 'A poor one, I suppose?'

'They arrived in three hired flies,' the butler remarked deferentially, as he handed a dish: 'they don't keep their own carriage, and the furniture's of the poorest.'

'Ah,' replied my mother, 'so much the better.'

My father gave her a chilly glance; she was silent.

Certainly the Princess Zasyekin could not be a rich woman; the lodge she had taken was so dilapidated and small and low-pitched that people, even moderately well-off in the world, would hardly have consented to occupy it. At the time, however, all this went in at one ear and out at the other. The princely title had very little effect on me; I had just been reading Schiller's *Robbers*.

II

I WAS in the habit of wandering about our garden every evening on the look-out for rooks. I had long cherished a hatred for those wary, sly, and rapacious birds. On the day of which I have been speaking, I went as usual into the garden, and after patrolling all the walks without success (the rooks knew me, and merely cawed spasmodically at a distance), I chanced to go close ow fence which separated our domain from the narrow strip of en stretching beyond the lodge to the right, and belonging to it. I was walking along, my eyes on the ground. Suddenly I heard a voice; I looked across the fence, and was thunderstruck. . . . I was confronted with a curious spectacle.

A few paces from me on the grass between the green raspberry bushes stood a tall slender girl in a striped pink dress, with a white kerchief on her head; four young men were close round her, and she was slapping them by turns on the forehead with those small grey flowers, the name of which I don't know, though they are well known to children; the flowers form little bags, and burst open with a pop when you strike them against anything hard. The young men presented their foreheads so eagerly, and in the gestures of the girl (I saw her in profile), there was something so fascinating, imperious, caressing, mocking, and charming, that I almost cried out with admiration and delight, and would, I thought, have given everything in the world on the spot only to have had those exquisite fingers strike me on the forehead. My gun slipped on to the grass, I forgot everything, I devoured with my eyes the graceful shape and neck and lovely arms and the slightly disordered fair hair under the white kerchief, and the half-closed clever eye, and the eyelashes and the soft cheek beneath them. . . .

'Young man, hey, young man,' said a voice suddenly near me: 'is it quite permissible to stare so at unknown young ladies?'

I started, I was struck dumb. . . . Near me, the other side of the fence, stood a man with close-cropped black hair, looking ironically at me. At the same instant the girl too turned towards me. . . . I caught sight of big grey eyes in a bright mobile face, and the whole face suddenly quivered and laughed, there was a flash of white teeth, a droll lifting of the eyebrows. . . . I crimsoned, picked up my gun from the ground, and pursued by a musical but not ill-natured laugh, fled to my own room, flung myself on the bed, and hid my face in my hands. My heart was fairly leaping; I was greatly ashamed and overjoyed; I felt an excitement I had never known before.

After a rest, I brushed my hair, washed, and went downstairs to tea. The image of the young girl floated before me, my heart was no longer leaping, but was full of a sort of sweet oppression.

'What's the matter?' my father asked me all at once: 'have you killed a rook?'

I was on the point of telling him all about it, but I checked myself, and merely smiled to myself. As I was going to bed, I rotated—I don't know why—three times on one leg, pomaded my hair, got into bed, and slept like a top all night. Before morning I woke up for an instant, raised my head, looked round me in ecstasy, and fell asleep again.

III

'HOW can I make their acquaintance?' was my first thought when I waked in the morning. I went out in the garden before morning tea, but I did not go too near the fence, and saw no one. After drinking tea, I walked several times up and down the street before the house, and looked into the windows from a distance. . . . I fancied her face at a curtain, and I hurried away in alarm.

'I must make her acquaintance, though,' I thought, pacing distractedly about the sandy plain that stretches before Neskutchny park . . . 'but how, that is the question.' I recalled the minutest details of our meeting yesterday; I had for some reason or other a particularly vivid recollection of how she had laughed at me. . . . But while I racked my brains, and made various plans, fate had already provided for me.

In my absence my mother had received from her new neighbour a letter on grey paper, sealed with brown wax, such as is only used in notices from the post-office or on the corks of bottles of cheap wine. In this letter, which was written in illiterate language and in a slovenly hand, the princess begged my mother to use her powerful influence in her behalf; my mother, in the words of the princess, was very intimate with persons of high position, upon whom her fortunes and her children's fortunes depended, as she had some very important business in hand. 'I address myself to you,' she wrote, 'as one gentlewoman to another gentlewoman, and for that reason am glad to avail myself of the opportunity.' Concluding, she begged my mother's permission to call upon her. I found my mother in an unpleasant state of indecision; my father was not at home, and she had no one of whom to ask advice. Not to answer a gentlewoman, and a princess into the bargain, was impossible. But my mother was in a difficulty as to how to answer her. To write a note in French struck her as unsuitable, and Russian spelling was not a strong point with my mother herself, and she was aware of it, and did not care to expose herself. She was overjoyed when I made my appearance, and at once told me to go round to the princess's, and to explain to her by word of mouth that my mother would always be glad to do her excellency any service within her powers, and begged her to come to see her at one o'clock. This unexpectedly rapid fulfilment of my secret desires both delighted and appalled me. I made no sign, however, of the perturbation which came over me, and as a preliminary step went to my own room to put on a new necktie and tail coat; at home I still wore short jackets and lay-down collars, much as I abominated them.

IV

IN the narrow and untidy passage of the lodge, which I entered with an involuntary tremor in all my limbs, I was met by an old grey-headed servant with a dark copper-coloured face, surly little pig's eyes, and such deep furrows on his forehead and temples as I had never beheld in my life. He was carrying a plate containing the spine of a herring that had been gnawed at; and shutting the door that led into the room with his foot, he jerked out, 'What do you want?'

'Is the Princess Zasyekin at home?' I inquired.

'Vonifaty!' a jarring female voice screamed from within.

The man without a word turned his back on me, exhibiting as he did so the extremely threadbare hindpart of his livery with a solitary reddish heraldic button on it; he put the plate down on the floor, and went away.

'Did you go to the police station?' the same female voice called again. The man muttered something in reply. 'Eh. . . . Has some one come?' I heard again. . . . 'The young gentleman from next door. Ask him in, then.'

'Will you step into the drawing-room?' said the servant, making his appearance once more, and picking up the plate from the floor. I mastered my emotions, and went into the drawing-room.

I found myself in a small and not over clean apartment, containing some poor furniture that looked as if it had been hurriedly set down where it stood. At the window in an easy-chair with a broken arm was sitting a woman of fifty, bareheaded and ugly, in an old green dress, and a striped worsted wrap about her neck. Her small black eyes fixed me like pins.

I went up to her and bowed.

'I have the honour of addressing the Princess Zasyekin?'

'I am the Princess Zasyekin; and you are the son of Mr. V.?'

'Yes. I have come to you with a message from my mother.'

'Sit down, please. Vonifaty, where are my keys, have you seen them?'

I communicated to Madame Zasyekin my mother's reply to her note. She heard me out, drumming with her fat red fingers on the window-pane, and when I had finished, she stared at me once more.

'Very good; I'll be sure to come,' she observed at last. 'But how young you are! How old are you, may I ask?'

'Sixteen,' I replied, with an involuntary stammer.

The princess drew out of her pocket some greasy papers covered with writing, raised them right up to her nose, and began looking through them.

'A good age,' she ejaculated suddenly, turning round restlessly on her chair. 'And do you, pray, make yourself at home. I don't stand on ceremony.'

'No, indeed,' I thought, scanning her unprepossessing person with a disgust I could not restrain.

At that instant another door flew open quickly, and in the doorway stood the girl I had seen the previous evening in the garden. She lifted her hand, and a mocking smile gleamed in her face.

'Here is my daughter,' observed the princess, indicating her with her elbow. 'Zinotchka, the son of our neighbour, Mr. V. What is your name, allow me to ask?'

'Vladimir,' I answered, getting up, and stuttering in my excitement.

'And your father's name?'

'Petrovitch.'

'Ah! I used to know a commissioner of police whose name was Vladimir Petrovitch too. Vonifaty! don't look for my keys; the keys are in my pocket.'

The young girl was still looking at me with the same smile, faintly fluttering her eyelids, and putting her head a little on one side.

'I have seen Monsieur Voldemar before,' she began. (The silvery note of her voice ran through me with a sort of sweet shiver.) 'You will let me call you so?'

'Oh, please,' I faltered.

'Where was that?' asked the princess.

The young princess did not answer her mother.

'Have you anything to do just now?' she said, not taking her eyes off me.

'Oh, no.'

'Would you like to help me wind some wool? Come in here, to me.'

She nodded to me and went out of the drawing-room. I followed her.

In the room we went into, the furniture was a little better, and was arranged with more taste. Though, indeed, at the moment, I was scarcely capable of noticing anything; I moved as in a dream and felt all through my being a sort of intense blissfulness that verged on imbecility.

The young princess sat down, took out a skein of red wool and, motioning me to a seat opposite her, carefully untied the skein and laid it across my hands. All this she did in silence with a sort of droll deliberation and with the same bright sly smile on her slightly parted lips. She began to wind the wool on a bent card, and all at once she dazzled me with a glance so brilliant and rapid, that I could not help dropping my eyes. When her eyes, which were generally half closed, opened to their full extent, her face was completely transfigured; it was as though it were flooded with light.

'What did you think of me yesterday, M'sieu Voldemar?' she asked after a brief pause. 'You thought ill of me, I expect?'

'I . . . princess . . . I thought nothing . . . how can I? . . .' I answered in confusion.

'Listen,' she rejoined. 'You don't know me yet. I'm a very strange person; I like always to be told the truth. You, I have just heard, are sixteen, and I am twenty-one: you see I'm a great deal older than you, and so you ought always to tell me the truth . . . and to do what I tell you,' she added. 'Look at me: why don't you look at me?'

I was still more abashed; however, I raised my eyes to her. She smiled, not her former smile, but a smile of approbation. 'Look at me,' she said, dropping her voice caressingly: 'I don't dislike that . . . I like your face; I have a presentiment we shall be friends. But do you like me?' she added slyly.

'Princess . . .' I was beginning.

'In the first place, you must call me Zinaïda Alexandrovna, and in the second place it's a bad habit for children'—(she corrected herself) 'for young people—not to say straight out what they feel. That's all very well for grown-up people. You like me, don't you?'

Though I was greatly delighted that she talked so freely to me, still I was a little hurt. I wanted to show her that she had not a mere boy to deal with, and assuming as easy and serious an air as I could, I observed, 'Certainly. I like you very much, Zinaïda Alexandrovna; I have no wish to conceal it.'

She shook her head very deliberately. 'Have you a tutor?' she asked suddenly.

'No; I've not had a tutor for a long, long while.'

I told a lie; it was not a month since I had parted with my Frenchman.

'Oh! I see then—you are quite grown-up.'

She tapped me lightly on the fingers. 'Hold your hands straight!' And she applied herself busily to winding the ball.

I seized the opportunity when she was looking down and fell to watching her, at first stealthily, then more and more boldly. Her face struck me as even more charming than on the previous evening; everything in it was so delicate, clever, and sweet. She was sitting with her back to a window covered with a white blind, the sunshine, streaming in through the blind, shed a soft light over her fluffy golden curls, her innocent neck, her sloping shoulders, and tender untroubled bosom. I gazed at her, and how dear and near she was already to me! It seemed to me I had known her a long while and had never known anything nor lived at all till I met her. . . . She was wearing a dark and rather shabby dress and an apron; I would gladly, I felt, have kissed every fold of that dress and apron. The tips of her little shoes peeped out from under her skirt; I could have bowed down in adoration to those shoes. . . . 'And here I am sitting before her,' I thought; 'I have made acquaintance with her . . . what happiness, my God!' I could hardly keep from jumping up from my chair in ecstasy, but I only swung my legs a little, like a small child who has been given sweetmeats.

I was as happy as a fish in water, and I could have stayed in that room for ever, have never left that place.

Her eyelids were slowly lifted, and once more her clear eyes shone kindly upon me, and again she smiled.

'How you look at me!' she said slowly, and she held up a threatening finger.

I blushed . . . 'She understands it all, she sees all,' flashed through my mind. 'And how could she fail to understand and see it all?'

All at once there was a sound in the next room—the clink of a sabre.

'Zina!' screamed the princess in the drawing-room, 'Byelovzorov has brought you a kitten.'

'A kitten!' cried Zinaïda, and getting up from her chair impetuously, she flung the ball of worsted on my knees and ran away.

I too got up and, laying the skein and the ball of wool on the window-sill, I went into the drawing-room and stood still, hesitating. In the middle of the room, a tabby kitten was lying with outstretched paws; Zinaïda was on her knees before it, cautiously lifting up its little face. Near the old princess, and filling up almost the whole space between the two windows, was a flaxen curly-headed young man, a hussar, with a rosy face and prominent eyes.

'What a funny little thing!' Zinaïda was saying; 'and its eyes are not grey, but green, and what long ears! Thank you, Viktor Yegoritch! you are very kind.'

The hussar, in whom I recognised one of the young men I had seen the evening before, smiled and bowed with a clink of his spurs and a jingle of the chain of his sabre.

'You were pleased to say yesterday that you wished to possess a tabby kitten with long ears . . . so I obtained it. Your word is law.' And he bowed again.

The kitten gave a feeble mew and began sniffing the ground.

'It's hungry!' cried Zinaïda. 'Vonifaty, Sonia! bring some milk.'

A maid, in an old yellow gown with a faded kerchief at her neck, came in with a saucer of milk and set it before the kitten. The kitten started, blinked, and began lapping.

'What a pink little tongue it has!' remarked Zinaïda, putting her head almost on the ground and peeping at it sideways under its very nose.

The kitten having had enough began to purr and move its paws affectedly. Zinaïda got up, and turning to the maid said carelessly, 'Take it away.'

'For the kitten—your little hand,' said the hussar, with a simper and a shrug of his strongly-built frame, which was tightly buttoned up in a new uniform.

'Both,' replied Zinaïda, and she held out her hands to him. While he was kissing them, she looked at me over his shoulder.

I stood stockstill in the same place and did not know whether to laugh, to say something, or to be silent. Suddenly through the open door into the passage I caught sight of our footman, Fyodor. He was making signs to me. Mechanically I went out to him.

'What do you want?' I asked.

'Your mamma has sent for you,' he said in a whisper. 'She is angry that you have not come back with the answer.'

'Why, have I been here long?'

'Over an hour.'

'Over an hour!' I repeated unconsciously, and going back to the drawing-room I began to make bows and scrape with my heels.

'Where are you off to?' the young princess asked, glancing at me from behind the hussar.

'I must go home. So I am to say,' I added, addressing the old lady, 'that you will come to us about two.'

'Do you say so, my good sir.'

The princess hurriedly pulled out her snuff-box and took snuff so loudly that I positively jumped. 'Do you say so,' she repeated, blinking tearfully and sneezing.

I bowed once more, turned, and went out of the room with that sensation of awkwardness in my spine which a very young man feels when he knows he is being looked at from behind.

'Mind you come and see us again, M'sieu Voldemar,' Zinaïda called, and she laughed again.

'Why is it she's always laughing?' I thought, as I went back home escorted by Fyodor, who said nothing to me, but walked behind me with an air of disapprobation. My mother scolded me and wondered what ever I could have been doing so long at the princess's. I made her no reply and went off to my own room. I felt suddenly very sad. . . . I tried hard not to cry. . . . I was jealous of the hussar.

V

THE princess called on my mother as she had promised and made a disagreeable impression on her. I was not present at their interview, but at table my mother told my father that this Princess Zasyekin struck her as a *femme très vulgaire*,[1] that she had quite worn her out begging her to interest Prince Sergei in their behalf, that she seemed to have no end of lawsuits and affairs on hand — *de vilaines affaires d'argent*[2] — and must be a very troublesome and litigious person. My mother added, however, that she had asked her and her daughter to dinner the next day (hearing the word 'daughter' I buried my nose in my plate), for after all she was a neighbour and a person of title. Upon this my father informed my mother that he remembered now who this lady was; that he had in his youth known the deceased Prince Zasyekin, a very well-bred, but frivolous and absurd person; that he had been nicknamed in society '*le Parisien,*' from having lived a long while in Paris; that he had been very rich, but had gambled away all his property; and for some unknown reason, probably for money, though indeed he might have chosen better, if so, my father added with a cold smile, he had

[1] *femme très vulgaire*] very common woman.
[2] *de vilaines affaires d'argent*] of ugly money matters.

married the daughter of an agent, and after his marriage had entered upon speculations and ruined himself utterly.

'If only she doesn't try to borrow money,' observed my mother.

'That's exceedingly possible,' my father responded tranquilly. 'Does she speak French?'

'Very badly.'

'H'm. It's of no consequence anyway. I think you said you had asked the daughter too; some one was telling me she was a very charming and cultivated girl.'

'Ah! Then she can't take after her mother.'

'Nor her father either,' rejoined my father. 'He was cultivated indeed, but a fool.'

My mother sighed and sank into thought. My father said no more. I felt very uncomfortable during this conversation.

After dinner I went into the garden, but without my gun. I swore to myself that I would not go near the Zasyekins' garden, but an irresistible force drew me thither, and not in vain. I had hardly reached the fence when I caught sight of Zinaïda. This time she was alone. She held a book in her hands, and was coming slowly along the path. She did not notice me.

I almost let her pass by; but all at once I changed my mind and coughed.

She turned round, but did not stop, pushed back with one hand the broad blue ribbon of her round straw hat, looked at me, smiled slowly, and again bent her eyes on the book.

I took off my cap, and after hesitating a moment, walked away with a heavy heart. '*Que suis-je pour elle?*'[3] I thought (God knows why) in French.

Familiar footsteps sounded behind me; I looked round, my father came up to me with his light, rapid walk.

'Is that the young princess?' he asked me.

'Yes.'

'Why, do you know her?'

'I saw her this morning at the princess's.'

My father stopped, and, turning sharply on his heel, went back. When he was on a level with Zinaïda, he made her a courteous bow. She, too, bowed to him, with some astonishment on her face, and dropped her book. I saw how she looked after him. My father was always irreproachably dressed, simple and in a style of his own; but his figure had never struck me as more graceful, never had his grey hat sat more becomingly on his curls, which were scarcely perceptibly thinner than they had once been.

I bent my steps toward Zinaïda, but she did not even glance at me; she picked up her book again and went away.

[3] '*Que suis-je pour elle?*'] 'What am I to her?'

VI

THE whole evening and the following day I spent in a sort of dejected apathy. I remember I tried to work and took up Keidanov, but the boldly printed lines and pages of the famous text-book passed before my eyes in vain. I read ten times over the words: 'Julius Caesar was distinguished by warlike courage.' I did not understand anything and threw the book aside. Before dinner-time I pomaded myself once more, and once more put on my tail-coat and necktie.

'What's that for?' my mother demanded. 'You're not a student yet, and God knows whether you'll get through the examination. And you've not long had a new jacket! You can't throw it away!'

'There will be visitors,' I murmured almost in despair.

'What nonsense! fine visitors indeed!'

I had to submit. I changed my tail-coat for my jacket, but I did not take off the necktie. The princess and her daughter made their appearance half an hour before dinner-time; the old lady had put on, in addition to the green dress with which I was already acquainted, a yellow shawl, and an old-fashioned cap adorned with flame-coloured ribbons. She began talking at once about her money difficulties, sighing, complaining of her poverty, and imploring assistance, but she made herself at home; she took snuff as noisily, and fidgeted and lolled about in her chair as freely as ever. It never seemed to have struck her that she was a princess. Zinaïda on the other hand was rigid, almost haughty in her demeanour, every inch a princess. There was a cold immobility and dignity in her face. I should not have recognised it; I should not have known her smiles, her glances, though I thought her exquisite in this new aspect too. She wore a light barége dress with pale blue flowers on it; her hair fell in long curls down her cheek in the English fashion; this style went well with the cold expression of her face. My father sat beside her during dinner, and entertained his neighbour with the finished and serene courtesy peculiar to him. He glanced at her from time to time, and she glanced at him, but so strangely, almost with hostility. Their conversation was carried on in French; I was surprised, I remember, at the purity of Zinaïda's accent. The princess, while we were at table, as before made no ceremony; she ate a great deal, and praised the dishes. My mother was obviously bored by her, and answered her with a sort of weary indifference; my father faintly frowned now and then. My mother did not like Zinaïda either. 'A conceited minx,' she said next day. 'And fancy, what she has to be conceited about, *avec sa mine de grisette!*'[1]

'It's clear you have never seen any grisettes,' my father observed to her.

[1] '*avec sa mine de grisette!*'] 'with her tramp's face!'

'Thank God, I haven't!'

'Thank God, to be sure . . . only how can you form an opinion of them, then?'

To me Zinaïda had paid no attention whatever. Soon after dinner the princess got up to go.

'I shall rely on your kind offices, Maria Nikolaevna and Piotr Vassilitch,' she said in a doleful sing-song to my mother and father. 'I've no help for it! There were days, but they are over. Here I am, an excellency, and a poor honour it is with nothing to eat!'

My father made her a respectful bow and escorted her to the door of the hall. I was standing there in my short jacket, staring at the floor, like a man under sentence of death. Zinaïda's treatment of me had crushed me utterly. What was my astonishment, when, as she passed me, she whispered quickly with her former kind expression in her eyes: 'Come to see us at eight, do you hear, be sure. . . .' I simply threw up my hands, but already she was gone, flinging a white scarf over her head.

VII

AT eight o'clock precisely, in my tail-coat and with my hair brushed up into a tuft on my head, I entered the passage of the lodge, where the princess lived. The old servant looked crossly at me and got up unwillingly from his bench. There was a sound of merry voices in the drawing-room. I opened the door and fell back in amazement. In the middle of the room was the young princess, standing on a chair, holding a man's hat in front of her; round the chair crowded some half a dozen men. They were trying to put their hands into the hat, while she held it above their heads, shaking it violently. On seeing me, she cried, 'Stay, stay, another guest, he must have a ticket too,' and leaping lightly down from the chair she took me by the cuff of my coat. 'Come along,' she said, 'why are you standing still? *Messieurs*, let me make you acquainted: this is M'sieu Voldemar, the son of our neighbour. And this,' she went on, addressing me, and indicating her guests in turn, 'Count Malevsky, Doctor Lushin, Meidanov the poet, the retired captain Nirmatsky, and Byelovzorov the hussar, whom you've seen already. I hope you will be good friends.'

I was so confused that I did not even bow to any one; in Doctor Lushin I recognised the dark man who had so mercilessly put me to shame in the garden; the others were unknown to me.

'Count!' continued Zinaïda, 'write M'sieu Voldemar a ticket.'

'That's not fair,' was objected in a slight Polish accent by the count, a very handsome and fashionably dressed brunette, with expressive brown eyes, a thin little white nose, and delicate little moustaches over a tiny mouth. 'This gentleman has not been playing forfeits with us.'

'It's unfair,' repeated in chorus Byelovzorov and the gentleman described as a retired captain, a man of forty, pock-marked to a hideous degree, curly-headed as a negro, round-shouldered, bandy-legged, and dressed in a military coat without epaulets, worn unbuttoned.

'Write him a ticket I tell you,' repeated the young princess. 'What's this mutiny? M'sieu Voldemar is with us for the first time, and there are no rules for him yet. It's no use grumbling—write it, I wish it.'

The count shrugged his shoulders but bowed submissively, took the pen in his white, ring-bedecked fingers, tore off a scrap of paper and wrote on it.

'At least let us explain to Mr. Voldemar what we are about,' Lushin began in a sarcastic voice, 'or else he will be quite lost. Do you see, young man, we are playing forfeits? the princess has to pay a forfeit, and the one who draws the lucky lot is to have the privilege of kissing her hand. Do you understand what I've told you?'

I simply stared at him, and continued to stand still in bewilderment, while the young princess jumped up on the chair again, and again began waving the hat. They all stretched up to her, and I went after the rest.

'Meidanov,' said the princess to a tall young man with a thin face, little dim-sighted eyes, and exceedingly long black hair, 'you as a poet ought to be magnanimous, and give up your number to M'sieu Voldemar so that he may have two chances instead of one.'

But Meidanov shook his head in refusal, and tossed his hair. After all the others I put my hand into the hat, and unfolded my lot. . . . Heavens! what was my condition when I saw on it the word, Kiss!

'Kiss!' I could not help crying aloud.

'Bravo! he has won it,' the princess said quickly. 'How glad I am!' She came down from the chair and gave me such a bright sweet look, that my heart bounded. 'Are you glad?' she asked me.

'Me?' . . . I faltered.

'Sell me your lot,' Byelovzorov growled suddenly just in my ear. 'I'll give you a hundred roubles.'

I answered the hussar with such an indignant look, that Zinaïda clapped her hands, while Lushin cried, 'He's a fine fellow!'

'But, as master of the ceremonies,' he went on, 'it's my duty to see that all the rules are kept. M'sieu Voldemar, go down on one knee. That is our regulation.'

Zinaïda stood in front of me, her head a little on one side as though to get a better look at me; she held out her hand to me with dignity. A mist passed before my eyes; I meant to drop on one knee, sank on both, and pressed my lips to Zinaïda's fingers so awkwardly that I scratched myself a little with the tip of her nail.

'Well done!' cried Lushin, and helped me to get up.

The game of forfeits went on. Zinaïda sat me down beside her. She invented all sorts of extraordinary forfeits! She had among other things to represent a 'statue,' and she chose as a pedestal the hideous Nirmatsky, told him to bow down in an arch, and bend his head down on his breast. The laughter never paused for an instant. For me, a boy constantly brought up in the seclusion of a dignified manor-house, all this noise and uproar, this unceremonious, almost riotous gaiety, these relations with unknown persons, were simply intoxicating. My head went round, as though from wine. I began laughing and talking louder than the others, so much so that the old princess, who was sitting in the next room with some sort of clerk from the Tversky gate, invited by her for consultation on business, positively came in to look at me. But I felt so happy that I did not mind anything, I didn't care a straw for any one's jeers, or dubious looks. Zinaïda continued to show me a preference, and kept me at her side. In one forfeit, I had to sit by her, both hidden under one silk handkerchief: I was to tell her *my secret*. I remember our two heads being all at once in a warm, half-transparent, fragrant darkness, the soft, close brightness of her eyes in the dark, and the burning breath from her parted lips, and the gleam of her teeth and the ends of her hair tickling me and setting me on fire. I was silent. She smiled slyly and mysteriously, and at last whispered to me, 'Well, what is it?' but I merely blushed and laughed, and turned away, catching my breath. We got tired of forfeits—we began to play a game with a string. My God! what were my transports when, for not paying attention, I got a sharp and vigorous slap on my fingers from her, and how I tried afterwards to pretend that I was absent-minded, and she teased me, and would not touch the hands I held out to her! What didn't we do that evening! We played the piano, and sang and danced and acted a gypsy encampment. Nirmatsky was dressed up as a bear, and made to drink salt water. Count Malevsky showed us several sorts of card tricks, and finished, after shuffling the cards, by dealing himself all the trumps at whist, on which Lushin 'had the honour of congratulating him.' Meidanov recited portions from his poem 'The Manslayer' (romanticism was at its height at this period), which he intended to bring out in a black cover with the title in blood-red letters; they stole the clerk's cap off his knee, and made him dance a Cossack dance by way of ransom for it; they dressed up old Vonifaty in a woman's cap, and the young princess put on a man's hat. . . . I could not enumerate all we did. Only Byelovzorov kept more and more in the background, scowling and angry. . . . Sometimes his eyes looked bloodshot, he flushed all over, and it seemed every minute as though he would rush out upon us all and scatter us like shavings in all directions; but the young princess would glance at him, and shake her finger at him, and he would retire into his corner again.

We were quite worn out at last. Even the old princess, though she was ready for anything, as she expressed it, and no noise wearied her, felt tired at last, and longed for peace and quiet. At twelve o'clock at night, supper was served, consisting of a piece of stale dry cheese, and some cold turnovers of minced ham, which seemed to me more delicious than any pastry I had ever tasted; there was only one bottle of wine, and that was a strange one; a dark-coloured bottle with a wide neck, and the wine in it was of a pink hue; no one drank it, however. Tired out and faint with happiness, I left the lodge; at parting Zinaïda pressed my hand warmly, and again smiled mysteriously.

The night air was heavy and damp in my heated face; a storm seemed to be gathering; black stormclouds grew and crept across the sky, their smoky outlines visibly changing. A gust of wind shivered restlessly in the dark trees, and somewhere, far away on the horizon, muffled thunder angrily muttered as it were to itself.

I made my way up to my room by the back stairs. My old man-nurse was asleep on the floor, and I had to step over him; he waked up, saw me, and told me that my mother had again been very angry with me, and had wished to send after me again, but that my father had prevented her. (I had never gone to bed without saying good-night to my mother, and asking her blessing. There was no help for it now!)

I told my man that I would undress and go to bed by myself, and I put out the candle. But I did not undress, and did not go to bed.

I sat down on a chair, and sat a long while, as though spell-bound. What I was feeling was so new and so sweet. . . . I sat still, hardly looking round and not moving, drew slow breaths, and only from time to time laughed silently at some recollection, or turned cold within at the thought that I was in love, that this was she, that this was love. Zinaïda's face floated slowly before me in the darkness — floated, and did not float away; her lips still wore the same enigmatic smile, her eyes watched me, a little from one side, with a questioning, dreamy, tender look . . . as at the instant of parting from her. At last I got up, walked on tiptoe to my bed, and without undressing, laid my head carefully on the pillow, as though I were afraid by an abrupt movement to disturb what filled my soul. . . . I lay down, but did not even close my eyes. Soon I noticed that faint glimmers of light of some sort were thrown continually into the room. . . . I sat up and looked at the window. The window-frame could be clearly distinguished from the mysteriously and dimly-lighted panes. It is a storm, I thought; and a storm it really was, but it was raging so very far away that the thunder could not be heard; only blurred, long, as it were branching, gleams of lightning flashed continually over the sky; it was not flashing, though, so much as quivering and twitching like the wing of a dying bird. I got up, went to the window, and stood there till morning. . . . The lightning never ceased for an instant; it was what is called among the peasants a *sparrow night*. I gazed at the dumb sandy plain, at the dark mass of the Neskutchny gardens, at the yellowish façades of the distant buildings, which seemed to quiver too at each faint flash. . . . I gazed, and could not turn away; these silent lightning flashes, these gleams seemed in response to the secret silent fires which were aglow within me. Morning began to dawn; the sky was flushed in patches of crimson. As the sun came nearer, the lightning grew gradually paler, and ceased; the quivering gleams were fewer and fewer, and vanished at last, drowned in the sobering positive light of the coming day. . . .

And my lightning flashes vanished too. I felt great weariness and peace . . . but Zinaïda's image still floated triumphant over my soul. But it too, this image, seemed more tranquil: like a swan rising out of the reeds of a bog, it stood out from the other unbeautiful figures surrounding it, and as I fell asleep, I flung myself before it in farewell, trusting adoration. . . .

Oh, sweet emotions, gentle harmony, goodness and peace of the softened heart, melting bliss of the first raptures of love, where are they, where are they?

VIII

THE next morning, when I came down to tea, my mother scolded me — less severely, however, than I had expected — and made me tell her how I had spent the previous evening. I answered her in few words, omitting many details, and trying to give the most innocent air to everything.

'Anyway, they're people who're not *comme il faut*,'[1] my mother commented, 'and you've no business to be hanging about there, instead of preparing yourself for the examination, and doing your work.'

As I was well aware that my mother's anxiety about my studies was confined to these few words, I did not feel it necessary to make any rejoinder; but after morning tea was over, my father took me by the arm, and turning into the garden with me, forced me to tell him all I had seen at the Zasyekins'.

A curious influence my father had over me, and curious were the relations existing between us. He took hardly any interest in my education, but he never hurt my feelings; he respected my freedom, he treated me — if I may so express it — with courtesy, . . . only he never let me be really close to him. I loved him, I admired him, he was my ideal of a man — and Heavens! how passionately devoted I should have been to him, if I had not been continually conscious of his holding me off! But when he liked, he could almost instantaneously, by a single word, a single gesture, call forth an unbounded confidence in him. My soul expanded, I chattered away to

[1] '*comme il faut*'] correct, proper.

him, as to a wise friend, a kindly teacher . . . then he as suddenly got rid of me, and again he was keeping me off, gently and affectionately, but still he kept me off.

Sometimes he was in high spirits, and then he was ready to romp and frolic with me, like a boy (he was fond of vigorous physical exercise of every sort); once — it never happened a second time! — he caressed me with such tenderness that I almost shed tears. . . . But high spirits and tenderness alike vanished completely, and what had passed between us, gave me nothing to build on for the future — it was as though I had dreamed it all. Sometimes I would scrutinise his clever handsome bright face . . . my heart would throb, and my whole being yearn to him . . . he would seem to feel what was going on within me, would give me a passing pat on the cheek, and go away, or take up some work, or suddenly freeze all over as only he knew how to freeze, and I shrank into myself at once, and turned cold too. His rare fits of friendliness to me were never called forth by my silent, but intelligible entreaties: they always occurred unexpectedly. Thinking over my father's character later, I have come to the conclusion that he had no thoughts to spare for me and for family life; his heart was in other things, and found complete satisfaction elsewhere. 'Take for yourself what you can, and don't be ruled by others; to belong to oneself—the whole savour of life lies in that,' he said to me one day. Another time, I, as a young democrat, fell to airing my views on liberty (he was 'kind,' as I used to call it, that day; and at such times I could talk to him as I liked). 'Liberty,' he repeated; 'and do you know what can give a man liberty?'

'What?'

'Will, his own will, and it gives power, which is better than liberty. Know how to will, and you will be free, and will lead.'

My father, before all, and above all, desired to live, and lived. . . . Perhaps he had a presentiment that he would not have long to enjoy the 'savour' of life; he died at forty-two.

I described my evening at the Zasyekins' minutely to my father. Half attentively, half carelessly, he listened to me, sitting on a garden seat, drawing in the sand with his cane. Now and then he laughed, shot bright, droll glances at me, and spurred me on with short questions and assents. At first I could not bring myself even to utter the name of Zinaïda, but I could not restrain myself long, and began singing her praises. My father still laughed; then he grew thoughtful, stretched, and got up.

I remembered that as he came out of the house he had ordered his horse to be saddled. He was a splendid horseman, and, long before Rarey, had the secret of breaking in the most vicious horses.

'Shall I come with you, father?' I asked.

'No,' he answered, and his face resumed its ordinary expression of friendly indifference. 'Go alone, if you like; and tell the coachman I'm not going.'

He turned his back on me and walked rapidly away. I looked after him; he disappeared through the gates. I saw his hat moving along beside the fence; he went into the Zasyekins'.

He stayed there not more than an hour, but then departed at once for the town, and did not return home till evening.

After dinner I went myself to the Zasyekins'. In the drawing-room I found only the old princess. On seeing me she scratched her head under her cap with a knitting-needle, and suddenly asked me, could I copy a petition for her.

'With pleasure,' I replied, sitting down on the edge of a chair.

'Only mind and make the letters bigger,' observed the princess, handing me a dirty sheet of paper; 'and couldn't you do it to-day, my good sir?'

'Certainly, I will copy it to-day.'

The door of the next room was just opened, and in the crack I saw the face of Zinaïda, pale and pensive, her hair flung carelessly back; she stared at me with big chilly eyes, and softly closed the door.

'Zina, Zina!' called the old lady. Zinaïda made no response. I took home the old lady's petition and spent the whole evening over it.

IX

MY 'passion' dated from that day. I felt at that time, I recollect, something like what a man must feel on entering the service: I had ceased now to be simply a young boy; I was in love. I have said that my passion dated from that day; I might have added that my sufferings too dated from the same day. Away from Zinaïda I pined; nothing was to my mind; everything went wrong with me; I spent whole days thinking intensely about her . . . I pined when away, . . . but in her presence I was no better off. I was jealous; I was conscious of my insignificance; I was stupidly sulky or stupidly abject, and, all the same, an invincible force drew me to her, and I could not help a shudder of delight whenever I stepped through the doorway of her room. Zinaïda guessed at once that I was in love with her, and indeed I never even thought of concealing it. She amused herself with my passion, made a fool of me, petted and tormented me. There is a sweetness in being the sole source, the autocratic and irresponsible cause of the greatest joy and profoundest pain to another, and I was like wax in Zinaïda's hands; though, indeed, I was not the only one in love with her. All the men who visited the house were crazy over her, and she kept them all in leading-strings at her feet. It amused her to arouse their hopes and then their fears, to turn them round her finger (she used to call it knocking their heads together), while they never dreamed of offering resistance and eagerly submitted to her. About her whole being, so full of life and beauty, there was a peculiarly bewitching mixture of slyness and carelessness, of artificiality and simplicity, of composure and frolicsomeness; about everything she did or said, about every action of hers, there clung a delicate, fine charm, in which an individual power was manifest at work. And her face was ever changing, working too; it expressed, almost at the same time, irony, dreaminess, and passion. Various emotions, delicate and quick-changing as the shadows of clouds on a sunny day of wind, chased one another continually over her lips and eyes.

Each of her adorers was necessary to her. Byelovzorov, whom she sometimes called 'my wild beast,' and sometimes simply 'mine,' would gladly have flung himself into the fire for her sake. With little confidence in his intellectual abilities and other qualities, he was for ever offering her marriage, hinting that the others were merely hanging about with no serious intention. Meidanov responded to the poetic fibres of her nature; a man of rather cold temperament, like almost all writers, he forced himself to convince her, and perhaps himself, that he adored her, sang her praises in endless verses, and read them to her with a peculiar enthusiasm, at once affected and sincere. She sympathised with him, and at the same time jeered at him a little; she had no great faith in him, and after listening to his outpourings, she would make him read Pushkin, as she said, to clear the air. Lushin, the ironical doctor, so cynical in words, knew her better than any of them, and loved her more than all, though he abused her to her face and behind her back. She could not help respecting him, but made him smart for it, and at times, with a peculiar, malignant pleasure, made him feel that he too was at her mercy. 'I'm a flirt, I'm heartless, I'm an actress in my instincts,' she said to him one day in my presence; 'well and good! Give me your hand then; I'll stick this pin in it, you'll be ashamed of this young man's seeing it, it will hurt you, but you'll laugh for all that, you truthful person.' Lushin crimsoned, turned away, bit his lips, but ended by submitting his hand. She pricked it, and he did in fact begin to laugh, . . . and she laughed, thrusting the pin in pretty deeply, and peeping into his eyes, which he vainly strove to keep in other directions. . . .

I understood least of all the relations existing between Zinaïda and Count Malevsky. He was handsome, clever, and adroit, but something equivocal, something false in him was apparent even to me, a boy of sixteen, and I marvelled that Zinaïda did not notice it. But possibly she did notice this element of falsity really and was not repelled by it. Her irregular education, strange acquaintances and habits, the constant presence of her mother, the poverty and disorder in their house, everything, from the very liberty the young girl enjoyed, with the consciousness of her superiority to the people around her, had developed in her a sort of half-contemptuous carelessness and lack of fastidiousness. At any time anything might happen; Vonifaty might announce that there was no sugar, or some revolting scandal would come to her ears, or her guests would fall to quarrelling among themselves—she would only shake her curls, and say, 'What does it matter?' and care little enough about it.

But my blood, anyway, was sometimes on fire with indignation when Malevsky approached her, with a sly, fox-like action, leaned gracefully on the back of her chair, and began whispering in her ear with a self-satisfied and ingratiating little smile, while she folded her arms across her bosom, looked intently at him and smiled too, and shook her head.

'What induces you to receive Count Malevsky?' I asked her one day.

'He has such pretty moustaches,' she answered. 'But that's rather beyond you.'

'You needn't think I care for him,' she said to me another time. 'No; I can't care for people I have to look down upon. I must have some one who can master me. . . . But, merciful heavens, I hope I may never come across any one like that! I don't want to be caught in any one's claws, not for anything.'

'You'll never be in love, then?'

'And you? Don't I love you?' she said, and she flicked me on the nose with the tip of her glove.

Yes, Zinaïda amused herself hugely at my expense. For three weeks I saw her every day, and what didn't she do with me! She rarely came to see us, and I was not sorry for it; in our house she was transformed into a young lady, a young princess, and I was a little overawed by her. I was afraid of betraying myself before my mother; she had taken a great dislike to Zinaïda, and kept a hostile eye upon us. My father I was not so much afraid of; he seemed not to notice me. He talked little to her, but always with special cleverness and significance. I gave up working and reading; I even gave up walking about the neighbourhood and riding my horse. Like a beetle tied by the leg, I moved continually round and round my beloved little lodge. I would gladly have stopped there altogether, it seemed . . . but that was impossible. My mother scolded me, and sometimes Zinaïda herself drove me away. Then I used to shut myself up in my room, or go down to the very end of the garden, and climbing into what was left of a tall stone greenhouse, now in ruins, sit for hours with my legs hanging over the wall that looked on to the road, gazing and gazing and seeing nothing. White butterflies flitted lazily by me, over the dusty nettles; a saucy sparrow settled not far off on the half crumbling red brickwork and twittered irritably, incessantly twisting and turning and preening his tail-feathers; the still mistrustful rooks cawed now and then, sitting high, high up on the bare top of a birch-tree; the sun and wind played softly on its pliant branches; the tinkle of the bells of the Don monastery floated across to me from time to time, peaceful and dreary; while I sat, gazed, listened, and was filled full of a nameless sensation in which all was contained: sadness and joy and the foretaste of the future, and the desire and dread of life. But at that time I understood nothing of it, and could have given a name to nothing of all that was passing at random within me, or should have called it all by one name — the name of Zinaïda.

Zinaïda continued to play cat and mouse with me. She flirted with me, and I was all agitation and rapture; then she would suddenly thrust me away, and I dared not go near her — dared not look at her.

I remember she was very cold to me for several days together; I was completely crushed, and creeping timidly to their lodge, tried to keep close to the old princess, regardless of the circumstance that she was particularly scolding and grumbling just at that time; her financial affairs had been going badly, and she had already had two 'explanations' with the police officials.

One day I was walking in the garden beside the familiar fence, and I caught sight of Zinaïda; leaning on both arms, she was sitting on the grass, not stirring a muscle. I was about to make off cautiously, but she suddenly raised her head and beckoned me imperiously. My heart failed me; I did not understand her at first. She repeated her signal. I promptly jumped over the fence and ran joyfully up to her, but she brought me to a halt with a look, and motioned me to the path two paces from her. In confusion, not knowing what to do, I fell on my knees at the edge of the path. She was so pale, such bitter suffering, such intense weariness, was expressed in every feature of her face, that it sent a pang to my heart, and I muttered unconsciously, 'What is the matter?'

Zinaïda stretched out her head, picked a blade of grass, bit it and flung it away from her.

'You love me very much?' she asked at last. 'Yes.'

I made no answer — indeed, what need was there to answer?

'Yes,' she repeated, looking at me as before. 'That's so. The same eyes,' — she went on; sank into thought, and hid her face in her hands. 'Everything's grown so loathsome to me,' she whispered, 'I would have gone to the other end of the world first — I can't bear it, I can't get over it. . . . And what is there before me! . . . Ah, I am wretched. . . . My God, how wretched I am!'

'What for?' I asked timidly.

Zinaïda made no answer, she simply shrugged her shoulders. I remained kneeling, gazing at her with intense sadness. Every word she had uttered simply cut me to the heart. At that instant I felt I would gladly have given my life, if only she should not grieve. I gazed at her — and though I could not understand why she was wretched, I vividly pictured to myself, how in a fit of insupportable anguish, she had suddenly come out into the garden, and sunk to the earth, as though mown down by a scythe. It was all bright and green about her; the wind was whispering in the leaves of the trees, and swinging now and then a long branch of a raspberry bush over Zinaïda's head. There was a sound of the cooing of doves, and the bees hummed, flying low over the scanty grass. Overhead the sun was radiantly blue—while I was so sorrowful. . . .

'Read me some poetry,' said Zinaïda in an undertone, and she propped herself on her elbow; 'I like your reading poetry. You read it in sing-song, but that's no matter, that comes of being young. Read me "On the Hills of Georgia." Only sit down first.'

I sat down and read 'On the Hills of Georgia.'

' "That the heart cannot choose but love," ' repeated Zinaïda. 'That's where poetry's so fine; it tells us what is not, and what's not only better than what is, but much more like the truth, "cannot choose but love,"—it might want not to, but it can't help it.' She was silent again, then all at once she started and got up. 'Come along. Meidanov's indoors with mamma, he brought me his poem, but I deserted him. His feelings are hurt too now . . . I can't help it! you'll understand it all some day . . . only don't be angry with me!'

Zinaïda hurriedly pressed my hand and ran on ahead. We went back into the lodge. Meidanov set to reading us his 'Manslayer,' which had just appeared in print, but I did not hear him. He screamed and drawled his four-foot iambic lines, the alternating rhythms jingled like little bells, noisy and meaningless, while I still watched Zinaïda and tried to take in the import of her last words.

'Perchance some unknown rival
Has surprised and mastered thee?'

Meidanov bawled suddenly through his nose—and my eyes and Zinaïda's met. She looked down and faintly blushed. I saw her blush, and grew cold with terror. I had been jealous before, but only at that instant the idea of her being in love flashed upon my mind. 'Good God! she is in love!'

X

MY real torments began from that instant. I racked my brains, changed my mind, and changed it back again, and kept an unremitting, though, as far as possible, secret watch on Zinaïda. A change had come over her, that was obvious. She began going walks alone—and long walks. Sometimes she would not see visitors; she would sit for hours together in her room. This had never been a habit of hers till now. I suddenly became—or fancied I had become—extraordinarily penetrating.

'Isn't it he? or isn't it he?' I asked myself, passing in inward agitation from one of her admirers to another. Count Malevsky secretly struck me as more to be feared than the others, though, for Zinaïda's sake, I was ashamed to confess it to myself.

My watchfulness did not see beyond the end of my nose, and its secrecy probably deceived no one; any way, Doctor Lushin soon saw through me. But he, too, had changed of late; he had grown thin, he laughed as often, but his laugh seemed more hollow, more spiteful, shorter, an involuntary nervous irritability took the place of his former light irony and assumed cynicism.

'Why are you incessantly hanging about here, young man?' he said to me one day, when we were left alone together in the Zasyekins' drawing-room. (The young princess had not come home from a walk, and the shrill voice of the old princess could be heard within; she was scolding the maid.) 'You ought to be studying, working—while you're young—and what are you doing?'

'You can't tell whether I work at home,' I retorted with some haughtiness, but also with some hesitation.

'A great deal of work you do! that's not what you're thinking about! Well, I won't find fault with that . . . at your age that's in the natural order of things. But you've been awfully unlucky in your choice. Don't you see what this house is?'

'I don't understand you,' I observed.

'You don't understand? so much the worse for you. I regard it as a duty to warn you. Old bachelors, like me, can come here, what harm can it do us! we're tough, nothing can hurt us, what harm can it do us; but your skin's tender yet—this air is bad for you—believe me, you may get harm from it.'

'How so?'

'Why, are you well now? Are you in a normal condition? Is what you're feeling—beneficial to you—good for you?'

'Why, what am I feeling?' I said, while in my heart I knew the doctor was right.

'Ah, young man, young man,' the doctor went on with an intonation that suggested that something highly insulting to me was contained in these two words, 'what's the use of your prevaricating, when, thank God, what's in your heart is in your face, so far? But there, what's the use of talking? I shouldn't come here myself, if . . . (the doctor compressed his lips) . . . if I weren't such a queer fellow. Only this is what surprises me; how it is, you, with your intelligence, don't see what is going on around you?'

'And what is going on?' I put in, all on the alert.

The doctor looked at me with a sort of ironical compassion.

'Nice of me!' he said as though to himself, 'as if he need know anything of it. In fact, I tell you again,' he added, raising his voice, 'the atmosphere here is not fit for you. You like being here, but what of that! it's nice and sweet-smelling in a greenhouse—but there's no living in it. Yes! do as I tell you, and go back to your Keidanov.'

The old princess came in, and began complaining to the doctor of her toothache. Then Zinaïda appeared.

'Come,' said the old princess, 'you must scold her, doctor. She's drinking iced water all day long; is that good for her, pray, with her delicate chest?'

'Why do you do that?' asked Lushin.

'Why, what effect could it have?'

'What effect? You might get a chill and die.'

'Truly? Do you mean it? Very well—so much the better.'

'A fine idea!' muttered the doctor. The old princess had gone out.

'Yes, a fine idea,' repeated Zinaïda. 'Is life such a festive affair? Just look about you. . . . Is it nice, eh? Or do you imagine I don't understand it, and don't feel it? It gives me pleasure—drinking iced water; and can you seriously assure me that such a life is worth too much to be risked for an instant's pleasure—happiness I won't even talk about.'

'Oh, very well,' remarked Lushin, 'caprice and irresponsibility. . . . Those two words sum you up; your whole nature's contained in those two words.'

Zinaïda laughed nervously.

'You're late for the post, my dear doctor. You don't keep a good look-out; you're behind the times. Put on your spectacles. I'm in no capricious humour now. To make fools of you, to make a fool of myself . . . much fun there is in that!—and as for irresponsibility. . . . M'sieu Voldemar,' Zinaïda added suddenly, stamping, 'don't make such a melancholy face. I can't endure people to pity me.' She went quickly out of the room.

'It's bad for you, very bad for you, this atmosphere, young man,' Lushin said to me once more.

XI

ON the evening of the same day the usual guests were assembled at the Zasyekins'. I was among them.

The conversation turned on Meidanov's poem. Zinaïda expressed genuine admiration of it. 'But do you know what?' she said to him. 'If I were a poet, I would choose quite different subjects. Perhaps it's all nonsense, but strange ideas sometimes come into my head, especially when I'm not asleep in the early morning, when the sky begins to turn rosy and grey both at once. I would, for instance . . . You won't laugh at me?'

'No, no!' we all cried, with one voice.

'I would describe,' she went on, folding her arms across her bosom and looking away, 'a whole company of young girls at night in a great boat, on a silent river. The moon is shining, and they are all in white, and wearing garlands of white flowers, and singing, you know, something in the nature of a hymn.'

'I see—I see; go on,' Meidanov commented with dreamy significance.

'All of a sudden, loud clamour, laughter, torches, tambourines on the bank. . . . It's a troop of Bacchantes dancing with songs and cries. It's your business to make a picture of it, Mr. Poet; . . . only I should like the torches to be red and to smoke a great deal, and the Bacchantes' eyes to gleam under their wreaths, and the wreaths to be dusky. Don't forget the tiger-skins, too, and goblets and gold—lots of gold. . . .'

'Where ought the gold to be?' asked Meidanov, tossing back his sleek hair and distending his nostrils.

'Where? on their shoulders and arms and legs—everywhere. They say in ancient times women wore gold rings on their ankles. The Bacchantes call the girls in the boat to them. The girls have ceased singing their hymn—they cannot go on with it, but they do not stir, the river carries them to the bank. And suddenly one of them slowly rises. . . . This you must describe nicely: how she slowly gets up in the moonlight, and how her companions are afraid. . . . She steps over the edge of the boat, the Bacchantes surround her, whirl her away into night and darkness. . . . Here put in smoke in clouds and everything in confusion. There is nothing but the sound of their shrill cry, and her wreath left lying on the bank.'

Zinaïda ceased. ('Oh! she is in love!' I thought again.)

'And is that all?' asked Meidanov.

'That's all.'

'That can't be the subject of a whole poem,' he observed pompously, 'but I will make use of your idea for a lyrical fragment.'

'In the romantic style?' queried Malevsky.

'Of course, in the romantic style—Byronic.'

'Well, to my mind, Hugo beats Byron,' the young count observed negligently; 'he's more interesting.'

'Hugo is a writer of the first class,' replied Meidanov; 'and my friend, Tonkosheev, in his Spanish romance, *El Trovador* . . .'

'Ah! is that the book with the question-marks turned upside down?' Zinaïda interrupted.

'Yes. That's the custom with the Spanish. I was about to observe that Tonkosheev . . .'

'Come! you're going to argue about classicism and romanticism again,' Zinaïda interrupted him a second time. 'We'd much better play . . .

'Forfeits?' put in Lushin.

'No, forfeits are a bore; at comparisons.' (This game Zinaïda had invented herself. Some object was mentioned, every one tried to compare it with something, and the one who chose the best comparison got a prize.)

She went up to the window. The sun was just setting; high up in the sky were large red clouds.

'What are those clouds like?' questioned Zinaïda; and without waiting for our answer, she said, 'I think they are like the purple sails on the golden ship of Cleopatra, when she sailed to meet Antony. Do you remember, Meidanov, you were telling me about it not long ago?'

All of us, like Polonius in *Hamlet*, opined that the clouds recalled nothing so much as those sails, and that not one of us could discover a better comparison.

'And how old was Antony then?' inquired Zinaïda.

'A young man, no doubt,' observed Malevsky.

'Yes, a young man,' Meidanov chimed in in confirmation.

'Excuse me,' cried Lushin, 'he was over forty.'

'Over forty,' repeated Zinaïda, giving him a rapid glance. . . .

I soon went home. 'She is in love,' my lips unconsciously repeated. . . . 'But with whom?'

XII

THE days passed by. Zinaïda became stranger and stranger, and more and more incomprehensible. One day I went over to her, and saw her sitting in a basket-chair, her head pressed to the sharp edge of the table. She drew herself up . . . her whole face was wet with tears.

'Ah, you!' she said with a cruel smile. 'Come here.'

I went up to her. She put her hand on my head, and suddenly catching hold of my hair began pulling it.

'It hurts me,' I said at last.

'Ah! does it? And do you suppose nothing hurts me?' she replied.

'Ai!' she cried suddenly, seeing she had pulled a little tuft of hair out. 'What have I done? Poor M'sieu Voldemar!'

She carefully smoothed the hair she had torn out, stroked it round her finger, and twisted it into a ring.

'I shall put your hair in a locket and wear it round my neck,' she said, while the tears still glittered in her eyes. 'That will be some small consolation to you, perhaps . . . and now good-bye.'

I went home, and found an unpleasant state of things there. My mother was having a scene with my father; she was reproaching him with something, while he, as his habit was, maintained a polite and chilly silence, and soon left her. I could not hear what my mother was talking of, and indeed I had no thought to spare for the subject; I only remember that when the interview was over, she sent for me to her room, and referred with great displeasure to the frequent visits I paid the princess, who was, in her words, *une femme capable de tout.*[1] I kissed her hand (this was what I always did when I wanted to cut short a conversation) and went off to my room. Zinaïda's tears had completely overwhelmed me; I positively did not know

[1] *une femme capable de tout*] a woman capable of anything.

what to think, and was ready to cry myself; I was a child after all, in spite of my sixteen years. I had now given up thinking about Malevsky, though Byelovzorov looked more and more threatening every day, and glared at the wily count like a wolf at a sheep; but I thought of nothing and of no one. I was lost in imaginings, and was always seeking seclusion and solitude. I was particularly fond of the ruined greenhouse. I would climb up on the high wall, and perch myself, and sit there, such an unhappy, lonely, and melancholy youth, that I felt sorry for myself—and how consolatory where those mournful sensations, how I revelled in them! . . .

One day I was sitting on the wall looking into the distance and listening to the ringing of the bells. . . . Suddenly something floated up to me—not a breath of wind and not a shiver, but as it were a whiff of fragrance—as it were, a sense of some one's being near. . . . I looked down. Below, on the path, in a light greyish gown, with a pink parasol on her shoulder, was Zinaïda, hurrying along. She caught sight of me, stopped, and pushing back the brim of her straw hat, she raised her velvety eyes to me.

'What are you doing up there at such a height?' she asked me with a rather queer smile. 'Come,' she went on, 'you always declare you love me; jump down into the road to me if you really do love me.'

Zinaïda had hardly uttered those words when I flew down, just as though some one had given me a violent push from behind. The wall was about fourteen feet high. I reached the ground on my feet, but the shock was so great that I could not keep my footing; I fell down, and for an instant fainted away. When I came to myself again, without opening my eyes, I felt Zinaïda beside me. 'My dear boy,' she was saying, bending over me, and there was a note of alarmed tenderness in her voice, 'how could you do it, dear; how could you obey? . . . You know I love you. . . . Get up.'

Her bosom was heaving close to me, her hands were caressing my head, and suddenly—what were my emotions at that moment—her soft, fresh lips began covering my face with kisses . . . they touched my lips. . . . But then Zinaïda probably guessed by the expression of my face that I had regained consciousness, though I still kept my eyes closed, and rising rapidly to her feet, she said: 'Come, get up, naughty boy, silly, why are you lying in the dust?' I got up. 'Give me my parasol,' said Zinaïda, 'I threw it down somewhere, and don't stare at me like that . . . what ridiculous nonsense! you're not hurt, are you? stung by the nettles, I daresay? Don't stare at me, I tell you. . . . But he doesn't understand, he doesn't answer,' she added, as though to herself. . . . 'Go home, M'sieu Voldemar, brush yourself, and don't dare to follow me, or I shall be angry, and never again . . .'

She did not finish her sentence, but walked rapidly away, while I sat down by the side of the road . . . my legs would not support me. The nettles had stung my hands, my back ached, and my head was giddy; but the feeling of rapture I experienced then has never come a second time in my life. It turned to a sweet ache in all my limbs and found expression at last in joyful hops and skips and shouts. Yes, I was still a child.

XIII

I WAS so proud and light-hearted all that day, I so vividly retained on my face the feeling of Zinaïda's kisses, with such a shudder of delight I recalled every word she had uttered, I so hugged my unexpected happiness that I felt positively afraid, positively unwilling to see her, who had given rise to these new sensations. It seemed to me that now I could ask nothing more of fate, that now I ought to 'go, and draw a deep last sigh and die.' But, next day, when I went into the lodge, I felt great embarrassment, which I tried to conceal under a show of modest confidence, befitting a man who wishes to make it apparent that he knows how to keep a secret. Zinaïda received me very simply, without any emotion, she simply shook her finger at me and asked me, whether I wasn't black and blue? All my modest confidence and air of mystery vanished instantaneously and with them my embarrassment. Of course, I had not expected anything particular, but Zinaïda's composure was like a bucket of cold water thrown over me. I realised that in her eyes I was a child, and was extremely miserable! Zinaïda walked up and down the room, giving me a quick smile, whenever she caught my eye, but her thoughts were far away, I saw that clearly. . . . 'Shall I begin about what happened yesterday myself,' I pondered; 'ask her, where she was hurrying off so fast, so as to find out once for all' . . . but with a gesture of despair, I merely went and sat down in a corner.

Byelovzorov came in; I felt relieved to see him.

'I've not been able to find you a quiet horse,' he said in a sulky voice; 'Freitag warrants one, but I don't feel any confidence in it, I am afraid.'

'What are you afraid of?' said Zinaïda; 'allow me to inquire?'

'What am I afraid of? Why, you don't know how to ride. Lord save us, what might happen! What whim is this has come over you all of a sudden?'

'Come, that's my business, Sir Wild Beast. In that case I will ask Piotr Vassilievitch.' . . . (My father's name was Piotr Vassilievitch. I was surprised at her mentioning his name so lightly and freely, as though she were confident of his readiness to do her a service.)

'Oh, indeed,' retorted Byelovzorov, 'you mean to go out riding with him then?'

'With him or with some one else is nothing to do with you. Only not with you, anyway.'

'Not with me,' repeated Byelovzorov. 'As you wish. Well, I shall find you a horse.'

'Yes, only mind now, don't send some old cow. I warn you I want to gallop.'

'Gallop away by all means . . . with whom is it, with Malevsky, you are going to ride?'

'And why not with him, Mr. Pugnacity? Come, be quiet,' she added, 'and don't glare. I'll take you too. You know that to my mind now Malevsky's — ugh!' She shook her head.

'You say that to console me,' growled Byelovzorov.

Zinaïda half closed her eyes. 'Does that console you? O . . . O . . . O . . . Mr. Pugnacity!' she said at last, as though she could find no other word. 'And you, M'sieu Voldemar, would you come with us?'

'I don't care to . . . in a large party,' I muttered, not raising my eyes.

'You prefer a *tête-à-tête*? . . . Well, freedom to the free, and heaven to the saints,' she commented with a sigh. 'Go along, Byelovzorov, and bestir yourself. I must have a horse for to-morrow.'

'Oh, and where's the money to come from?' put in the old princess.

Zinaïda scowled.

'I won't ask you for it; Byelovzorov will trust me.'

'He'll trust you, will he?' . . . grumbled the old princess, and all of a sudden she screeched at the top of her voice, 'Duniashka!'

'Maman, I have given you a bell to ring,' observed Zinaïda.

'Duniashka!' repeated the old lady.

Byelovzorov took leave; I went away with him. Zinaïda did not try to detain me.

XIV

THE next day I got up early, cut myself a stick, and set off beyond the town-gates. I thought I would walk off my sorrow. It was a lovely day, bright and not too hot, a fresh sportive breeze roved over the earth with temperate rustle and frolic, setting all things a-flutter and harassing nothing. I wandered a long while over hills and through woods; I had not felt happy, I had left home with the intention of giving myself up to melancholy, but youth, the exquisite weather, the fresh air, the pleasure of rapid motion, the sweetness of repose, lying on the thick grass in a solitary nook, gained the upper hand; the memory of those never-to-be-forgotten words, those kisses, forced itself once more upon my soul. It was sweet to me to think that Zinaïda could not, anyway, fail to do justice to my courage, my heroism. . . . 'Others may seem better to her than I,' I mused, 'let them! But others only say what they would do, while I have done it. And what more would I not do for her?' My fancy set to work. I began picturing to myself how I would save her from the hands of enemies; how, covered with blood I would tear her by force from prison, and expire at her feet. I remembered a picture hanging in our drawing-room — Malek-Adel bearing away Matilda — but at that point my attention was absorbed by the appearance of a speckled woodpecker who climbed busily up the slender stem of a birch-tree and peeped out uneasily from behind it, first to the right, then to the left, like a musician behind the bass-viol.

Then I sang 'Not the white snows,' and passed from that to a song well known at that period: 'I await thee, when the wanton zephyr,' then I began reading aloud Yermak's address to the stars from Homyakov's tragedy. I made an attempt to compose something myself in a sentimental vein, and invented the line which was to conclude each verse: 'O Zinaïda, Zinaïda!' but could get no further with it. Meanwhile it was getting on towards dinner-time. I went down into the valley; a narrow sandy path winding through it led to the town. I walked along this path. . . . The dull thud of horses' hoofs resounded behind me. I looked round instinctively, stood still and took off my cap. I saw my father and Zinaïda. They were riding side by side. My father was saying something to her, bending right over to her, his hand propped on the horses' neck, he was smiling. Zinaïda listened to him in silence, her eyes severely cast down, and her lips tightly pressed together. At first I saw them only; but a few instants later, Byelovzorov came into sight round a bend in the glade, he was wearing a hussar's uniform with a pelisse, and riding a foaming black horse. The gallant horse tossed its head, snorted and pranced from side to side, his rider was at once holding him in and spurring him on. I stood aside. My father gathered up the reins, moved away from Zinaïda, she slowly raised her eyes to him, and both galloped off. . . . Byelovzorov flew after them, his sabre clattering behind him. 'He's as red as a crab,' I reflected, 'while she . . . why's she so pale? out riding the whole morning, and pale?'

I redoubled my pace, and got home just at dinner-time. My father was already sitting by my mother's chair, dressed for dinner, washed and fresh; he was reading an article from the *Journal des Débats* in his smooth musical voice; but my mother heard him without attention, and when she saw me, asked where I had been to all day long, and added that she didn't like this gadding about God knows where, and God knows in what company. 'But I have been walking alone,' I was on the point of replying, but I looked at my father, and for some reason or other held my peace.

XV

FOR the next five or six days I hardly saw Zinaïda; she said she was ill, which did not, however, prevent the usual visitors from calling at the lodge to pay — as they expressed it, their duty — all, that is, except Meidanov, who promptly grew dejected and sulky when he had not an opportunity of being enthusiastic. Byelovzorov sat sullen and red-faced in a corner, buttoned up to the throat; on the refined face of Malevsky there flickered continually an evil smile; he had really fallen into disfavour with Zinaïda, and waited with special assiduity on the old princess, and even went with her in a hired coach to call on the Governor-General. This expedition turned out unsuccessful, however, and even led to an unpleasant experience for Malevsky; he was reminded of some scandal to do with certain officers of the engineers, and was forced in his explanations to plead his youth and inexperience at the time. Lushin came twice a day, but did not stay long; I was rather afraid of him after our last unreserved conversation, and at the same time felt a genuine attraction to him. He went a walk with me one day in the Neskutchny gardens, was very good-natured and nice, told me the names and properties of various plants and flowers, and suddenly, *à propos* of nothing at all, cried, hitting himself on his forehead, 'And I, poor fool, thought her a flirt! it's clear self-sacrifice is sweet for some people!'

'What do you mean by that?' I inquired.

'I don't mean to tell you anything,' Lushin replied abruptly.

Zinaïda avoided me; my presence—I could not help noticing it—affected her disagreeably. She involuntarily turned away from me . . . involuntarily; that was what was so bitter, that was what crushed me! But there was no help for it, and I tried not to cross her path, and only to watch her from a distance, in which I was not always successful. As before, something incomprehensible was happening to her; her face was different, she was different altogether. I was specially struck by the change that had taken place in her one warm still evening. I was sitting on a low garden bench under a spreading elderbush; I was fond of that nook; I could see from there the window of Zinaïda's room. I sat there; over my head a little bird was busily hopping about in the darkness of the leaves; a grey cat, stretching herself at full length, crept warily about the garden, and the first beetles were heavily droning in the air, which was still clear, though it was not light. I sat and gazed at the window, and waited to see if it would open; it did open, and Zinaïda appeared at it. She had on a white dress, and she herself, her face, shoulders, and arms, were pale to whiteness. She stayed a long while without moving, and looked out straight before her from under her knitted brows. I had never known such a look on her. Then she clasped her hands tightly, raised them to her lips, to her forehead, and suddenly pulling her fingers apart, she pushed back her hair behind her ears, tossed it, and with a sort of determination nodded her head, and slammed-to the window.

Three days later she met me in the garden. I was turning away, but she stopped me of herself.

'Give me your arm,' she said to me with her old affectionateness, 'it's a long while since we have had a talk together.'

I stole a look at her; her eyes were full of a soft light, and her face seemed as it were smiling through a mist.

'Are you still not well?' I asked her.

'No, that's all over now,' she answered, and she picked a small red rose. 'I am a little tired, but that too will pass off.'

'And will you be as you used to be again?' I asked.

Zinaïda put the rose up to her face, and I fancied the reflection of its bright petals had fallen on her cheeks. 'Why, am I changed?' she questioned me.

'Yes, you are changed,' I answered in a low voice.

'I have been cold to you, I know,' began Zinaïda, 'but you mustn't pay attention to that . . . I couldn't help it. . . . Come, why talk about it!'

'You don't want me to love you, that's what it is!' I cried gloomily, in an involuntary outburst.

'No, love me, but not as you did.'

'How then?'

'Let us be friends—come now!' Zinaïda gave me the rose to smell. 'Listen, you know I'm much older than you—I might be your aunt, really; well, not your aunt, but an older sister. And you . . .'

'You think me a child,' I interrupted.

'Well, yes, a child, but a dear, good clever one, whom I love very much. Do you know what? From this day forth I confer on you the rank of page to me; and don't you forget that pages have to keep close to their ladies. Here is the token of your new dignity,' she added, sticking the rose in the buttonhole of my jacket, 'the token of my favour.'

'I once received other favours from you,' I muttered.

'Ah!' commented Zinaïda, and she gave me a sidelong look, 'What a memory he has! Well? I'm quite ready now . . .' And stooping to me, she imprinted on my forehead a pure, tranquil kiss.

I only looked at her, while she turned away, and saying, 'Follow me, my page,' went into the lodge. I followed her—all in amazement. 'Can this gentle, reasonable girl,' I thought, 'be the Zinaïda I used to know?' I fancied her very walk was quieter, her whole figure statelier and more graceful . . .

And, mercy! with what fresh force love burned within me!

XVI

AFTER dinner the usual party assembled again at the lodge, and the young princess came out to them. All were there in full force, just as on that first evening which I never forgot; even Nirmatsky had limped to see her; Meidanov came this time earliest of all, he brought some new verses. The games of forfeits began again, but without the strange pranks, the practical jokes and noise—the gipsy element had vanished. Zinaïda gave a different tone to the proceedings. I sat beside her by virtue of my office as page. Among other things, she proposed that any one who had to pay a forfeit should tell his dream; but this was not successful. The dreams were either uninteresting (Byelovzorov had dreamed that he fed his mare on carp, and that she had a wooden head), or unnatural and invented. Meidanov regaled us with a regular romance; there were sepulchres in it, and angels with lyres, and talking flowers and music wafted from afar. Zinaïda did not let him finish. 'If we are to have compositions,' she said, 'let every one tell something made up, and no pretence about it.' The first who had to speak was again Byelovzorov.

The young hussar was confused. 'I can't make up anything!' he cried.

'What nonsense!' said Zinaïda. 'Well, imagine, for instance, you are married, and tell us how you would treat your wife. Would you lock her up?'

'Yes, I should lock her up.'

'And would you stay with her yourself?'

'Yes, I should certainly stay with her myself.'

'Very good. Well, but if she got sick of that, and she deceived you?'

'I should kill her.'

'And if she ran away?'

'I should catch her up and kill her all the same.'

'Oh. And suppose now I were your wife, what would you do then?'

Byelovzorov was silent a minute. 'I should kill myself. . . .'

Zinaïda laughed. 'I see yours is not a long story.'

The next forfeit was Zinaïda's. She looked at the ceiling and considered. 'Well, listen,' she began at last, 'what I have thought of. . . . Picture to yourselves a magnificent palace, a summer night, and a marvellous ball. This ball is given by a young queen. Everywhere gold and marble, crystal, silk, lights, diamonds, flowers, fragrant scents, every caprice of luxury.'

'You love luxury?' Lushin interposed.

'Luxury is beautiful,' she retorted; 'I love everything beautiful.'

'More than what is noble?' he asked.

'That's something clever, I don't understand it. Don't interrupt me. So the ball is magnificent. There are crowds of guests, all of them are young, handsome, and brave, all are frantically in love with the queen.'

'Are there no women among the guests?' queried Malevsky.

'No—or wait a minute—yes, there are some.'

'Are they all ugly?'

'No, charming. But the men are all in love with the queen. She is tall and graceful; she has a little gold diadem on her black hair.'

I looked at Zinaïda, and at that instant she seemed to me so much above all of us, there was such bright intelligence, and such power about her unruffled brows, that I thought: 'You are that queen!'

'They all throng about her,' Zinaïda went on, 'and all lavish the most flattering speeches upon her.'

'And she likes flattery?' Lushin queried.

'What an intolerable person! he keeps interrupting . . . who doesn't like flattery?'

'One more last question,' observed Malevsky, has the queen a husband?'

'I hadn't thought about that. No, why should she have a husband?'

'To be sure,' assented Malevsky, 'why should she have a husband?'

'*Silence!*' cried Meidanov in French, which he spoke very badly.

'*Merci!*' Zinaïda said to him. 'And so the queen hears their speeches, and hears the music, but does not look at one of the guests. Six windows are open from top to bottom, from floor to ceiling, and beyond them is a dark sky with big stars, a dark garden with big trees. The queen gazes out into the garden. Out there among the trees is a fountain; it is white in the darkness, and rises up tall, tall as an apparition. The queen hears, through the talk and the music, the soft splash of its waters. She gazes and thinks: you are all, gentlemen, noble, clever, and rich, you crowd round me, you treasure every word I utter, you are all ready to die at my feet, I hold you in my power . . . but out there, by the fountain, by that splashing water, stands and waits he whom I love, who holds me in his power. He has neither rich raiment nor precious stones, no one knows him, but he awaits me, and is certain I shall come—and I shall come—and there is no power that could stop me when I want to go out to him, and to stay with him, and be lost with him out there in the darkness of the garden, under the whispering of the trees, and the splash of the fountain . . .' Zinaïda ceased.

'Is that a made-up story?' Malevsky inquired slyly. Zinaïda did not even look at him.

'And what should we have done, gentlemen?' Lushin began suddenly, 'if we had been among the guests, and had known of the lucky fellow at the fountain?'

'Stop a minute, stop a minute,' interposed Zinaïda, 'I will tell you myself what each of you would have done. You, Byelovzorov, would have challenged him to a duel; you, Meidanov, would have written an epigram on him. . . . No, though, you can't write epigrams, you would have made up a long poem on him in the style of Barbier, and would have inserted your production in the *Telegraph*. You, Nirmatsky, would have borrowed . . . no, you would have lent him money at high interest; you, doctor, . . .' she stopped. 'There, I really don't know what you would have done. . . .'

'In the capacity of court physician,' answered Lushin, 'I would have advised the queen not to give balls when she was not in the humour for entertaining her guests. . . .'

'Perhaps you would have been right. And you, Count? . . .'

'And I?' repeated Malevsky with his evil smile. . . .

'You would offer him a poisoned sweetmeat.'

Malevsky's face changed slightly, and assumed for an instant a Jewish expression, but he laughed directly.

'And as for you, Voldemar, . . .' Zinaïda went on, 'but that's enough, though; let us play another game.'

'M'sieu Voldemar, as the queen's page, would have held up her train when she ran into the garden,' Malevsky remarked malignantly.

I was crimson with anger, but Zinaïda hurriedly laid a hand on my shoulder, and getting up, said in a rather shaky voice: 'I have never given your excellency the right to be rude, and therefore I will ask you to leave us.' She pointed to the door.

'Upon my word, princess,' muttered Malevsky, and he turned quite pale.

'The princess is right,' cried Byelovzorov, and he too rose.

'Good God, I'd not the least idea,' Malevsky went on, 'in my words there was nothing, I think, that could . . . I had no notion of offending you. . . . Forgive me.'

Zinaïda looked him up and down coldly, and coldly smiled. 'Stay, then, certainly,' she pronounced with a careless gesture of her arm. 'M'sieu Voldemar and I were needlessly incensed. It is your pleasure to sting . . . may it do you good.'

'Forgive me,' Malevsky repeated once more; while I, my thoughts dwelling on Zinaïda's gesture, said to myself again that no real queen could with greater dignity have shown a presumptuous subject to the door.

The game of forfeits went on for a short time after this little scene; every one felt rather ill at ease, not so much on account of this scene, as from another, not quite definite, but oppressive feeling. No one spoke of it, but every one was conscious of it in himself and in his neighbour. Meidanov read us his verses; and Malevsky praised them with exaggerated warmth. 'He wants to show how good he is now,' Lushin whispered to me. We soon broke up. A mood of reverie seemed to have come upon Zinaïda; the old princess sent word that she had a headache; Nirmatsky began to complain of his rheumatism. . . .

I could not for a long while get to sleep. I had been impressed by Zinaïda's story. 'Can there have been a hint in it?' I asked myself: 'and at whom and at what was she hinting? And if there really is anything to hint at . . . how is one to make up one's mind? No, no, it can't be,' I whispered, turning over from one hot cheek on to the other. . . . But I remembered the expression of Zinaïda's face during her story. . . . I remembered the exclamation that had broken from Lushin in the Neskutchny gardens, the sudden change in her behaviour to me, and I was lost in conjectures. 'Who is he?' These three words seemed to stand before my eyes traced upon the darkness; a lowering malignant cloud seemed hanging over me, and I felt its oppressiveness, and waited for it to break. I had grown used to many things of late; I had learned much from what I had seen at the Zasyekins; their disorderly ways, tallow candle-ends, broken knives and forks, grumpy Vonifaty, and shabby maidservants, the manners of the old princess—all their strange mode of life no longer struck me. . . . But what I was dimly discerning now in Zinaïda, I could never get used to. . . . 'An adventuress!' my mother had said of her one day. An adventuress—she, my idol, my divinity? This word stabbed me, I tried to get away from it into my pillow, I was indignant—and at the same time what would I not have agreed to, what would I not have given only to be that lucky fellow at the fountain! . . . My blood was on fire and boiling within me. 'The garden . . . the fountain,' I mused. . . . 'I will go into the garden.' I dressed quickly and slipped out of the house. The night was dark, the trees scarcely whispered, a soft chill air breathed down from the sky, a smell of fennel trailed across from the kitchen garden. I went through all the walks; the light sound of my own footsteps at once confused and emboldened me; I stood still, waited and heard my heart beating fast and loudly. At last I went up to the fence and leaned against the thin bar. Suddenly, or was it my fancy, a woman's figure flashed by, a few paces from me . . . I strained my eyes eagerly into the darkness, I held my breath. What was that? Did I hear steps, or was it my heart beating again? 'Who is here?' I faltered, hardly audibly. What was that again, a smothered laugh . . . or a rustling in the leaves . . . or a sigh just at my ear? I felt afraid . . . 'Who is here?' I repeated still more softly.

The air blew in a gust for an instant; a streak of fire flashed across the sky; it was a star falling. 'Zinaïda?' I wanted to call, but the word died away on my lips. And all at once everything became profoundly still around, as is often the case in the middle of the night. . . . Even the grasshoppers ceased their churr in the trees—only a window rattled somewhere. I stood and stood, and then went back to my room, to my chilled bed. I felt a strange sensation; as though I had gone to a tryst, and had been left lonely, and had passed close by another's happiness.

XVII

THE following day I only had a passing glimpse of Zinaïda: she was driving somewhere with the old princess in a cab. But I saw Lushin, who, however, barely vouchsafed me a greeting, and Malevsky. The young count grinned, and began affably talking to me. Of all those who visited at the lodge, he alone had succeeded in forcing his way into our house, and had favourably impressed my mother. My father did not take to him, and treated him with a civility almost insulting.

'Ah, *monsieur le page*,' began Malevsky, 'delighted to meet you. What is your lovely queen doing?'

His fresh handsome face was so detestable to me at that moment, and he looked at me with such contemptuous amusement that I did not answer him at all.

'Are you still angry?' he went on. 'You've no reason to be. It wasn't I who called you a page, you know, and pages attend queens especially. But allow me to remark that you perform your duties very badly.'

'How so?'

'Pages ought to be inseparable from their mistresses; pages ought to know everything they do, they ought, indeed, to watch over them,' he added, lowering his voice, 'day and night.'

'What do you mean?'

'What do I mean? I express myself pretty clearly, I fancy. Day and night. By day it's not so much matter; it's light, and people are about in the daytime; but by night, then look out for misfortune. I advise you not to sleep at nights and to watch, watch with all your energies. You remember, in the garden, by night, at the fountain, that's where there's need to look out. You will thank me.'

Malevsky laughed and turned his back on me. He, most likely, attached no great importance to what he had said to me, he had a reputation for mystifying, and was noted for his power of taking people in at masquerades, which was greatly augmented by the almost unconscious falsity in which his whole nature was steeped. . . . He only wanted to tease me; but every word he uttered was a poison that ran through my veins. The blood rushed to my head. 'Ah! so that's it!' I said to myself; 'good! So there was reason for me to feel drawn into the garden! That shan't be so!' I cried aloud, and struck myself on the chest with my fist, though precisely what should not be so I could not have said. 'Whether Malevsky himself goes into the garden,' I thought (he was bragging, perhaps; he has insolence enough for that), 'or some one else (the fence of our garden was very low, and there was no difficulty in getting over it), anyway, if any one falls into my hands, it will be the worse for him! I don't advise any one to meet me! I will prove to all the world and to her, the traitress (I actually used the word 'traitress') that I can be revenged!'

I returned to my own room, took out of the writing-table an English knife I had recently bought, felt its sharp edge, and knitting my brows with an air of cold and concentrated determination, thrust it into my pocket, as though doing such deeds was nothing out of the way for me, and not the first time. My heart heaved angrily, and felt heavy as a stone. All day long I kept a scowling brow and lips tightly compressed, and was continually walking up and down, clutching, with my hand in my pocket, the knife, which was warm from my grasp, while I prepared myself beforehand for something terrible. These new unknown sensations so occupied and even delighted me, that I hardly thought of Zinaïda herself. I was continually haunted by

Aleko, the young gipsy—'Where art thou going, young handsome man? Lie there,' and then, 'thou art all besprent with blood. . . . Oh, what hast thou done? . . . Naught!' With what a cruel smile I repeated that 'Naught!' My father was not at home; but my mother, who had for some time past been in an almost continual state of dumb exasperation, noticed my gloomy and heroic aspect, and said to me at supper, 'Why are you sulking like a mouse in a meal-tub?' I merely smiled condescendingly in reply, and thought, 'If only they knew!' It struck eleven; I went to my room, but did not undress; I waited for midnight; at last it struck. 'The time has come!' I muttered between my teeth; and buttoning myself up to the throat, and even pulling my sleeves up, I went into the garden.

I had already fixed on the spot from which to keep watch. At the end of the garden, at the point where the fence, separating our domain from the Zasyekins', joined the common wall, grew a pine-tree, standing alone. Standing under its low thick branches, I could see well, as far as the darkness of the night permitted, what took place around. Close by, ran a winding path which had always seemed mysterious to me; it coiled like a snake under the fence, which at that point bore traces of having been climbed over, and led to a round arbour formed of thick acacias. I made my way to the pine-tree, leaned my back against its trunk, and began my watch.

The night was as still as the night before, but there were fewer clouds in the sky, and the outlines of bushes, even of tall flowers, could be more distinctly seen. The first moments of expectation were oppressive, almost terrible. I had made up my mind to everything. I only debated how to act; whether to thunder, 'Where goest thou? Stand! show thyself—or death!' or simply to strike. . . . Every sound, every whisper and rustle, seemed to me portentous and extraordinary. . . . I prepared myself. . . . I bent forward. . . . But half-an-hour passed, an hour passed; my blood had grown quieter, colder; the consciousness that I was doing all this for nothing, that I was even a little absurd, that Malevsky had been making fun of me, began to steal over me. I left my ambush, and walked all about the garden. As if to taunt me, there was not the smallest sound to be heard anywhere; everything was at rest. Even our dog was asleep, curled up into a ball at the gate. I climbed up into the ruins of the greenhouse, saw the open country far away before me, recalled my meeting with Zinaïda, and fell to dreaming. . . .

I started. . . . I fancied I heard the creak of a door opening, then the faint crack of a broken twig. In two bounds I got down from the ruin, and stood still, all aghast. Rapid, light, but cautious footsteps sounded distinctly in the garden. They were approaching me. 'Here he is . . . here he is, at last!' flashed through my heart. With spasmodic haste, I pulled the knife out of my pocket; with spasmodic haste, I opened it. Flashes of red were whirling before my eyes; my hair stood up on my head in my fear and fury. . . . The steps were coming straight towards me; I bent—I craned forward to meet him. . . . A man came into view. . . . My God! it was my father!

I recognised him at once, though he was all muffled up in a dark cloak, and his hat was pulled down over his face. On tip-toe he walked by. He did not notice me, though nothing concealed me; but I was so huddled up and shrunk together that I fancy I was almost on the level of the ground. The jealous Othello, ready for murder, was suddenly transformed into a school-boy. . . . I was so taken aback by my father's unexpected appearance that for the first moment I did not notice where he had come from or in what direction he disappeared. I only drew myself up, and thought, 'Why is it my father is walking about in the garden at night?' when everything was still again. In my horror I had dropped my knife in the grass, but I did not even attempt to look for it; I was very much ashamed of myself. I was completely sobered at once. On my way to the house, however, I went up to my seat under the elder-tree, and looked up at Zinaïda's window. The small slightly-convex panes of the window shone dimly blue in the faint light thrown on them by the night sky. All at once—their colour began to change. . . . Behind them—I saw this, saw it distinctly—softly and cautiously a white blind was let down, let down right to the window-frame, and so stayed.

'What is that for?' I said aloud almost involuntarily when I found myself once more in my room. 'A dream, a chance, or . . .' The suppositions which suddenly rushed into my head were so new and strange that I did not dare to entertain them.

XVIII

I GOT up in the morning with a headache. My emotion of the previous day had vanished. It was replaced by a dreary sense of blankness and a sort of sadness I had not known till then, as though something had died in me.

'Why is it you're looking like a rabbit with half its brain removed?' said Lushin on meeting me. At lunch I stole a look first at my father, then at my mother: he was composed, as usual; she was, as usual, secretly irritated. I waited to see whether my father would make some friendly remarks to me, as he sometimes did. . . . But he did not even bestow his everyday cold greeting upon me. 'Shall I tell Zinaïda all?' I wondered. . . . 'It's all the same, anyway; all is at an end between us.' I went to see her, but told her nothing, and, indeed, I could not even have managed to get a talk with her if I had wanted to. The old princess's son, a cadet of twelve years old, had come from Petersburg for his holidays; Zinaïda at once handed her brother over to me. 'Here,' she said, 'my dear Volodya,'—it was the first time she had used this pet-name to me—'is a companion for you. His name is Volodya, too. Please, like him; he is still shy, but he has a good heart. Show him Neskutchny gardens, go walks with him, take him under your protection.

You'll do that, won't you? you're so good, too!' She laid both her hands affectionately on my shoulders, and I was utterly bewildered. The presence of this boy transformed me, too, into a boy. I looked in silence at the cadet, who stared as silently at me. Zinaïda laughed, and pushed us towards each other. 'Embrace each other, children!' We embraced each other. 'Would you like me to show you the garden?' I inquired of the cadet. 'If you please,' he replied, in the regular cadet's hoarse voice. Zinaïda laughed again. . . . I had time to notice that she had never had such an exquisite colour in her face before. I set off with the cadet. There was an old-fashioned swing in our garden. I sat him down on the narrow plank seat, and began swinging him. He sat rigid in his new little uniform of stout cloth, with its broad gold braiding, and kept tight hold of the cords. 'You'd better unbutton your collar,' I said to him. 'It's all right; we're used to it,' he said, and cleared his throat. He was like his sister. The eyes especially recalled her. I liked being nice to him; and at the same time an aching sadness was gnawing at my heart. 'Now I certainly am a child,' I thought; 'but yesterday. . . .' I remembered where I had dropped my knife the night before, and looked for it. The cadet asked me for it, picked a thick stalk of wild parsley, cut a pipe out of it, and began whistling. Othello whistled too.

But in the evening how he wept, this Othello, in Zinaïda's arms, when, seeking him out in a corner of the garden, she asked him why he was so depressed. My tears flowed with such violence that she was frightened. 'What is wrong with you? What is it, Volodya?' she repeated; and seeing I made no answer, and did not cease weeping, she was about to kiss my wet cheek. But I turned away from her, and whispered through my sobs, 'I know all. Why did you play with me? . . . What need had you of my love?'

'I am to blame, Volodya . . .' said Zinaïda. 'I am very much to blame . . .' she added, wringing her hands. 'How much there is bad and black and sinful in me! . . . But I am not playing with you now. I love you; you don't even suspect why and how. . . . But what is it you know?'

What could I say to her? She stood facing me, and looked at me; and I belonged to her altogether from head to foot directly she looked at me. . . . A quarter of an hour later I was running races with the cadet and Zinaïda. I was not crying, I was laughing, though my swollen eyelids dropped a tear or two as I laughed. I had Zinaïda's ribbon round my neck for a cravat, and I shouted with delight whenever I succeeded in catching her round the waist. She did just as she liked with me.

XIX

I SHOULD be in a great difficulty, if I were forced to describe exactly what passed within me in the course of the week after my unsuccessful midnight expedition. It was a strange feverish time, a sort of chaos, in which the most violently opposed feelings, thoughts, suspicions, hopes, joys, and sufferings, whirled together in a kind of hurricane. I was afraid to look into myself, if a boy of sixteen ever can look into himself; I was afraid to take stock of anything; I simply hastened to live through every day till evening; and at night I slept . . . the light-heartedness of childhood came to my aid. I did not want to know whether I was loved, and I did not want to acknowledge to myself that I was not loved; my father I avoided—but Zinaïda I could not avoid. . . . I burnt as in a fire in her presence . . . but what did I care to know what the fire was in which I burned and melted—it was enough that it was sweet to burn and melt. I gave myself up to all my passing sensations, and cheated myself, turning away from memories, and shutting my eyes to what I foreboded before me. . . . This weakness would not most likely have lasted long in any case . . . a thunderbolt cut it all short in a moment, and flung me into a new track altogether.

Coming in one day to dinner from a rather long walk, I learnt with amazement that I was to dine alone, that my father had gone away and my mother was unwell, did not want any dinner, and had shut herself up in her bedroom. From the faces of the footmen, I surmised that something extraordinary had taken place. . . . I did not dare to cross-examine them, but I had a friend in the young waiter Philip, who was passionately fond of poetry, and a performer on the guitar. I addressed myself to him. From him I learned that a terrible scene had taken place between my father and mother (and every word had been overheard in the maids' room; much of it had been in French, but Masha the lady's-maid had lived five years with a dressmaker from Paris, and she understood it all); that my mother had reproached my father with infidelity, with an intimacy with the young lady next door, that my father at first had defended himself, but afterwards had lost his temper, and he too had said something cruel, 'reflecting on her age,' which had made my mother cry; that my mother too had alluded to some loan which it seemed had been made to the old princess, and had spoken very ill of her and of the young lady too, and that then my father had threatened her. 'And all the mischief,' continued Philip, 'came from an anonymous letter; and who wrote it, no one knows, or else there'd have been no reason whatever for the matter to have come out at all.'

'But was there really any ground,' I brought out with difficulty, while my hands and feet went cold, and a sort of shudder ran through my inmost being.

Philip winked meaningly. 'There was. There's no hiding those things; for all that your father was careful this time—but there, you see, he'd, for instance, to hire a carriage or something . . . no getting on without servants, either.'

I dismissed Philip, and fell on to my bed. I did not sob, I did not give myself up to despair; I did not ask myself when and how this had happened;

I did not wonder how it was I had not guessed it before, long ago; I did not even upbraid my father. . . . What I had learnt was more than I could take in; this sudden revelation stunned me. . . . All was at an end. All the fair blossoms of my heart were roughly plucked at once, and lay about me, flung on the ground, and trampled underfoot.

XX

MY mother next day announced her intention of returning to the town. In the morning my father had gone into her bedroom, and stayed there a long while alone with her. No one had overheard what he said to her; but my mother wept no more; she regained her composure, and asked for food, but did not make her appearance nor change her plans. I remember I wandered about the whole day, but did not go into the garden, and never once glanced at the lodge, and in the evening I was the spectator of an amazing occurrence: my father conducted Count Malevsky by the arm through the dining-room into the hall, and, in the presence of a footman, said icily to him: 'A few days ago your excellency was shown the door in our house; and now I am not going to enter into any kind of explanation with you, but I have the honour to announce to you that if you ever visit me again, I shall throw you out of the window. I don't like your handwriting.' The count bowed, bit his lips, shrank away, and vanished.

Preparations were beginning for our removal to town, to Arbaty Street, where we had a house. My father himself probably no longer cared to remain at the country house; but clearly he had succeeded in persuading my mother not to make a public scandal. Everything was done quietly, without hurry; my mother even sent her compliments to the old princess, and expressed her regret that she was prevented by indisposition from seeing her again before her departure. I wandered about like one possessed, and only longed for one thing, for it all to be over as soon as possible. One thought I could not get out of my head: how could she, a young girl, and a princess too, after all, bring herself to such a step, knowing that my father was not a free man, and having an opportunity of marrying, for instance, Byelovzorov? What did she hope for? How was it she was not afraid of ruining her whole future? Yes, I thought, this is love, this is passion, this is devotion . . . and Lushin's words came back to me: to sacrifice oneself for some people is sweet. I chanced somehow to catch sight of something white in one of the windows of the lodge. . . . 'Can it be Zinaïda's face?' I thought . . . yes, it really was her face. I could not restrain myself. I could not part from her without saying a last good-bye to her. I seized a favourable instant, and went into the lodge.

In the drawing-room the old princess met me with her usual slovenly and careless greetings.

'How's this, my good man, your folks are off in such a hurry?' she observed, thrusting snuff into her nose. I looked at her, and a load was taken off my heart. The word 'loan,' dropped by Philip, had been torturing me. She had no suspicion . . . at least I thought so then. Zinaïda came in from the next room, pale, and dressed in black, with her hair hanging loose; she took me by the hand without a word, and drew me away with her.

'I heard your voice,' she began, 'and came out at once. Is it so easy for you to leave us, bad boy?'

'I have come to say good-bye to you, princess,' I answered, 'probably for ever. You have heard, perhaps, we are going away.'

Zinaïda looked intently at me.

'Yes, I have heard. Thanks for coming. I was beginning to think I should not see you again. Don't remember evil against me. I have sometimes tormented you, but all the same I am not what you imagine me.'

She turned away, and leaned against the window.

'Really, I am not like that. I know you have a bad opinion of me.'

'I?'

'Yes, you . . . you.'

'I?' I repeated mournfully, and my heart throbbed as of old under the influence of her overpowering, indescribable fascination. 'I? Believe me, Zinaïda Alexandrovna, whatever you did, however you tormented me, I should love and adore you to the end of my days.'

She turned with a rapid motion to me, and flinging wide her arms, embraced my head, and gave me a warm and passionate kiss. God knows whom that long farewell kiss was seeking, but I eagerly tasted its sweetness. I knew that it would never be repeated. 'Good-bye, good-bye,' I kept saying . . .

She tore herself away, and went out. And I went away. I cannot describe the emotion with which I went away. I should not wish it ever to come again; but I should think myself unfortunate had I never experienced such an emotion.

We went back to town. I did not quickly shake off the past; I did not quickly get to work. My wound slowly began to heal; but I had no ill-feeling against my father. On the contrary he had, as it were, gained in my eyes . . . let psychologists explain the contradiction as best they can. One day I was walking along a boulevard, and to my indescribable delight, I came across Lushin. I liked him for his straightforward and unaffected character, and besides he was dear to me for the sake of the memories he aroused in me. I rushed up to him. 'Aha!' he said, knitting his brows, 'so it's you, young man. Let me have a look at you. You're still as yellow as ever, but yet there's not the same nonsense in your eyes. You look like a man, not a lap-dog. That's good. Well, what are you doing? working?'

I gave a sigh. I did not like to tell a lie, while I was ashamed to tell the truth.

'Well, never mind,' Lushin went on, 'don't be shy. The great thing is to lead a normal life, and not be the slave of your passions. What do you get if not? Wherever you are carried by the tide—it's all a bad look-out; a man must stand on his own feet, if he can get nothing but a rock to stand on. Here, I've got a cough . . . and Byelovzorov—have you heard anything of him?'

'No. What is it?'

'He's lost, and no news of him; they say he's gone away to the Caucasus. A lesson to you, young man. And it's all from not knowing how to part in time, to break out of the net. You seem to have got off very well. Mind you don't fall into the same snare again. Good-bye.'

'I shan't,' I thought. . . . 'I shan't see her again.' But I was destined to see Zinaïda once more.

XXI

MY father used every day to ride out on horseback. He had a splendid English mare, a chestnut piebald, with a long slender neck and long legs, an inexhaustible and vicious beast. Her name was Electric. No one could ride her except my father. One day he came up to me in a good humour, a frame of mind in which I had not seen him for a long while; he was getting ready for his ride, and had already put on his spurs. I began entreating him to take me with him.

'We'd much better have a game of leap-frog,' my father replied. 'You'll never keep up with me on your cob.'

'Yes, I will; I'll put on spurs too.'

'All right, come along then.'

We set off. I had a shaggy black horse, strong, and fairly spirited. It is true it had to gallop its utmost, when Electric went at full trot, still I was not left behind. I have never seen any one ride like my father; he had such a fine carelessly easy seat, that it seemed that the horse under him was conscious of it, and proud of its rider. We rode through all the boulevards, reached the 'Maidens' Field,' jumped several fences (at first I had been afraid to take a leap, but my father had a contempt for cowards, and I soon ceased to feel fear), twice crossed the river Moskva, and I was under the impression that we were on our way home, especially as my father of his own accord observed that my horse was tired, when suddenly he turned off away from me at the Crimean ford, and galloped along the river-bank. I rode after him. When he had reached a high stack of old timber, he slid quickly off Electric, told me to dismount, and giving me his horse's bridle, told me to wait for him there at the timber-stack, and, turning off into a small street, disappeared. I began walking up and down the river-bank, leading the horses, and scolding Electric, who kept pulling, shaking her head, snorting and neighing as she went; and when I stood still, never failed to paw the ground, and whining, bite my cob on the neck; in fact she conducted herself altogether like a spoilt thorough-bred. My father did not come back. A disagreeable damp mist rose from the river; a fine rain began softly blowing up, and spotting with tiny dark flecks the stupid grey timber-stack, which I kept passing and repassing, and was deadly sick of by now. I was terribly bored, and still my father did not come. A sort of sentry-man, a Fin, grey all over like the timber, and with a huge old-fashioned shako, like a pot, on his head, and with a halberd (and how ever came a sentry, if you think of it, on the banks of the Moskva!) drew near, and turning his wrinkled face, like an old woman's, towards me, he observed, 'What are you doing here with the horses, young master? Let me hold them.'

I made him no reply. He asked me for tobacco. To get rid of him (I was in a fret of impatience, too), I took a few steps in the direction in which my father had disappeared, then walked along the little street to the end, turned the corner, and stood still. In the street, forty paces from me, at the open window of a little wooden house, stood my father, his back turned to me; he was leaning forward over the window-sill, and in the house, half hidden by a curtain, sat a woman in a dark dress talking to my father; this woman was Zinaïda.

I was petrified. This, I confess, I had never expected. My first impulse was to run away. 'My father will look round,' I thought, 'and I am lost . . .' but a strange feeling—a feeling stronger than curiosity, stronger than jealousy, stronger even than fear—held me there. I began to watch; I strained my ears to listen. It seemed as though my father were insisting on something. Zinaïda would not consent. I seem to see her face now—mournful, serious, lovely, and with an inexpressible impress of devotion, grief, love, and a sort of despair—I can find no other word for it. She uttered monosyllables, not raising her eyes, simply smiling—submissively, but without yielding. By that smile alone, I should have known my Zinaïda of old days. My father shrugged his shoulders, and straightened his hat on his head, which was always a sign of impatience with him. . . . Then I caught the words: '*Vous devez vous séparer de cette* . . .'[1] Zinaïda sat up, and stretched out her arm. . . . Suddenly, before my very eyes, the impossible happened. My father suddenly lifted the whip, with which he had been switching the dust off his coat, and I heard a sharp blow on that arm, bare to the elbow. I could scarcely restrain myself from crying out; while Zinaïda shuddered, looked without a word at my father, and slowly raising her arm to her lips, kissed the streak of red upon it. My father flung away the whip, and running

[1] '*Vous devez vous séparer de cette* . . .'] 'You ought to free yourself from that . . .'

quickly up the steps, dashed into the house. . . . Zinaïda turned round, and with outstretched arms and downcast head, she too moved away from the window.

My heart sinking with panic, with a sort of awe-struck horror, I rushed back, and running down the lane, almost letting go my hold of Electric, went back to the bank of the river. I could not think clearly of anything. I knew that my cold and reserved father was sometimes seized by fits of fury; and all the same, I could never comprehend what I had just seen. . . . But I felt at the time that, however long I lived, I could never forget the gesture, the glance, the smile, of Zinaïda; that her image, this image so suddenly presented to me, was imprinted for ever on my memory. I stared vacantly at the river, and never noticed that my tears were streaming. 'She is beaten,' I was thinking, . . . 'beaten . . . beaten. . . .'

'Hullo! what are you doing? Give me the mare!' I heard my father's voice saying behind me.

Mechanically I gave him the bridle. He leaped on to Electric . . . the mare, chill with standing, reared on her haunches, and leaped ten feet away . . . but my father soon subdued her; he drove the spurs into her sides, and gave her a blow on the neck with his fist. . . . 'Ah, I've no whip,' he muttered.

I remembered the swish and fall of the whip, heard so short a time before, and shuddered.

'Where did you put it?' I asked my father, after a brief pause.

My father made no answer, and galloped on ahead. I overtook him. I felt that I must see his face.

'Were you bored waiting for me?' he muttered through his teeth.

'A little. Where did you drop your whip?' I asked again.

My father glanced quickly at me. 'I didn't drop it,' he replied; 'I threw it away.' He sank into thought, and dropped his head . . . and then, for the first, and almost for the last time, I saw how much tenderness and pity his stern features were capable of expressing.

He galloped on again, and this time I could not overtake him; I got home a quarter-of-an-hour after him.

'That's love,' I said to myself again, as I sat at night before my writing-table, on which books and papers had begun to make their appearance; 'that's passion! . . . To think of not revolting, of bearing a blow from any one whatever . . . even the dearest hand! But it seems one can, if one loves. . . . While I . . . I imagined . . .'

I had grown much older during the last month; and my love, with all its transports and sufferings, struck me myself as something small and childish and pitiful beside this other unimagined something, which I could hardly fully grasp, and which frightened me like an unknown, beautiful, but menacing face, which one strives in vain to make out clearly in the half-darkness. . . .

A strange and fearful dream came to me that same night. I dreamed I went into a low dark room. . . . My father was standing with a whip in his hand, stamping with anger; in the corner crouched Zinaïda, and not on her arm, but on her forehead, was a stripe of red . . . while behind them both towered Byelovzorov, covered with blood; he opened his white lips, and wrathfully threatened my father.

Two months later, I entered the university; and within six months my father died of a stroke in Petersburg, where he had just moved with my mother and me. A few days before his death he received a letter from Moscow which threw him into a violent agitation. . . . He went to my mother to beg some favour of her: and, I was told, he positively shed tears—he, my father! On the very morning of the day when he was stricken down, he had begun a letter to me in French. 'My son,' he wrote to me, 'fear the love of woman; fear that bliss, that poison. . . .' After his death, my mother sent a considerable sum of money to Moscow.

XXII

FOUR years passed. I had just left the university, and did not know exactly what to do with myself, at what door to knock; I was hanging about for a time with nothing to do. One fine evening I met Meidanov at the theatre. He had got married, and had entered the civil service; but I found no change in him. He fell into ecstasies in just the same superfluous way, and just as suddenly grew depressed again.

'You know,' he told me among other things, 'Madame Dolsky's here.'

'What Madame Dolsky?'

'Can you have forgotten her?—the young Princess Zasyekin whom we were all in love with, and you too. Do you remember at the country-house near Neskutchny gardens?'

'She married a Dolsky?'

'Yes.'

'And is she here, in the theatre?'

'No: but she's in Petersburg. She came here a few days ago. She's going abroad.'

'What sort of fellow is her husband?' I asked.

'A splendid fellow, with property. He's a colleague of mine in Moscow. You can well understand—after the scandal . . . you must know all about it . . .' (Meidanov smiled significantly) 'it was no easy task for her to make a good marriage; there were consequences . . . but with her cleverness, everything is possible. Go and see her; she'll be delighted to see you. She's prettier than ever.'

Meidanov gave me Zinaïda's address. She was staying at the Hotel Demut. Old memories were astir within me. . . . I determined next day to go to see my former 'flame.' But some business happened to turn up; a week passed, and then another, and when at last I went to the Hotel Demut and asked for Madame Dolsky, I learnt that four days before, she had died, almost suddenly, in childbirth.

I felt a sort of stab at my heart. The thought that I might have seen her, and had not seen her, and should never see her—that bitter thought stung me with all the force of overwhelming reproach. 'She is dead!' I repeated, staring stupidly at the hall-porter. I slowly made my way back to the street, and walked on without knowing myself where I was going. All the past swam up and rose at once before me. So this was the solution, this was the goal to which that young, ardent, brilliant life had striven, all haste and agitation! I mused on this; I fancied those dear features, those eyes, those curls—in the narrow box, in the damp underground darkness—lying here, not far from me—while I was still alive, and, maybe, a few paces from my father. . . . I thought all this; I strained my imagination, and yet all the while the lines:

> 'From lips indifferent of her death I heard,
> Indifferently I listened to it, too,'

were echoing in my heart. O youth, youth! little dost thou care for anything; thou art master, as it were, of all the treasures of the universe—even sorrow gives thee pleasure, even grief thou canst turn to thy profit; thou art self-confident and insolent; thou sayest, 'I alone am living—look you!'—but thy days fly by all the while, and vanish without trace or reckoning; and everything in thee vanishes, like wax in the sun, like snow. . . . And, perhaps, the whole secret of thy charm lies, not in being able to do anything, but in being able to think thou wilt do anything; lies just in thy throwing to the winds, forces which thou couldst not make other use of; in each of us gravely regarding himself as a prodigal, gravely supposing that he is justified in saying, 'Oh, what might I not have done if I had not wasted my time!'

I, now . . . what did I hope for, what did I expect, what rich future did I foresee, when the phantom of my first love, rising up for an instant, barely called forth one sigh, one mournful sentiment?

And what has come to pass of all I hoped for? And now, when the shades of evening begin to steal over my life, what have I left fresher, more precious, than the memories of the storm—so soon over—of early morning, of spring?

But I do myself injustice. Even then, in those light-hearted young days, I was not deaf to the voice of sorrow, when it called upon me, to the solemn strains floating to me from beyond the tomb. I remember, a few days after I heard of Zinaïda's death, I was present, through a peculiar, irresistible impulse, at the death of a poor old woman who lived in the same house as we. Covered with rags, lying on hard boards, with a sack under her head, she died hardly and painfully. Her whole life had been passed in the bitter struggle with daily want; she had known no joy, had not tasted the honey of happiness. One would have thought, surely she would rejoice at death, at her deliverance, her rest. But yet, as long as her decrepit body held out, as long as her breast still heaved in agony under the icy hand weighing upon it, until her last forces left her, the old woman crossed herself, and kept whispering, 'Lord, forgive my sins'; and only with the last spark of consciousness, vanished from her eyes the look of fear, of horror of the end. And I remember that then, by the death-bed of that poor old woman, I felt aghast for Zinaïda, and longed to pray for her, for my father—and for myself.